W9-BXS-925

FINDING LOVE
FOR LINDSAY

FINDING LOVE FOR LINDSAY

•

Shelley Galloway

AVALON BOOKS
NEW YORK

Published by Thomas Bouregy & Co., Inc.
160 Madison Avenue, New York, NY 10016

Library of Congress Cataloging-in-Publication Data

Galloway, Shelley.
  Finding Love for Lindsay / Shelley Galloway.
  ISBN 0-8034-9803-9 (acid-free paper)
        p.   cm.
  I. Title.

PS3607.A42F556 2006
813'.6—dc22

2006024265

PRINTED IN THE UNITED STATES OF AMERICA
ON ACID-FREE PAPER
BY HADDON CRAFTSMEN, BLOOMSBURG, PENNSYLVANIA

To my girlfriends at Hallmark. Thanks for your encouragement, and for asking for more books in this series.

Chapter One

"Lindsay, you got a minute?"

Remembering that she'd just added "learn to relax during my morning walk" to her to-do list, Lindsay slowed her steps reluctantly. Rarely did anyone's "minute" ever take less than five or ten.

But it wasn't Annie's fault that Lindsay was more than a little stressed about her job.

Summoning up a smile, she said, "As a matter of fact, I do have a minute."

Annie's full cheeks beamed. "I'm kind of surprised to hear that, if you want to know the truth. You were practically jogging down the sidewalk."

"I just walk fast, always have," Lindsay replied, realizing with some discomfort that her efforts to stroll weren't getting very far. "What's going on?"

"I was curious about your stage company. What play are you going to put on next? Are there going to be tryouts anytime soon?"

The question pushed away any semblance of relaxation and pulled all work-related worries back to the forefront. Still reeling from the success of *Scrooge,* doing her best to find her place in the small town of Payton, and feeling pressured to produce another top-notch production, Lindsay Flynn felt she was doing her best to live day by day. Eyeing Annie Kilman a little more closely, she said, "I'm not sure. But, it's nice of you to ask."

"I'm afraid I'm not asking just to be nice. I want a part in it. Would you like me to send you the tape from *Footloose?* I was in the chorus in that last year."

"I saw that. Payton High sure does great productions," Lindsay replied sincerely just as the familiar knot appeared back in her stomach. She just wasn't ready to start fending off questions about her next big thing. And Annie, she suddenly realized, was not the least bit shy about pressuring her. "Well. Anyway. I haven't decided anything yet for the next production, but when I do—"

"What are you not sure about? The play or the tryouts?" Annie had never been one for evasive maneuvers.

Dare she say both? Her stomach clenched again, this time adding a little sting of acid reflux into the mix. If she wasn't careful, she was going to get an ulcer, just as her doctor had warned. "Actually, I'll have to get back to you about that. I haven't decided on a play yet."

Annie pushed her glasses up a little on the bridge of her nose. "But the article in the *Payton Registrar* claimed you were getting ready to organize things as soon as possible. That's not the case?"

No, that hadn't been the case at all. Actually, she'd been pretty surprised to read in the paper that she was so organized and motivated. Surprised and more than a little dismayed. "The *Registrar* kind of jumped the gun. It's only been a few months since *Scrooge.*"

"Seven. It's July, you know."

Lindsay knew. "I promise I'll let you know just as soon as things start happening."

Annie raised an eyebrow. "Gee, thanks."

"No problem."

As Annie wandered down the street, Lindsay's own steps slowed once again, though she was now completely worried—all thought of enjoying a leisurely morning walk forgotten. It really was time to put things into action again.

After *Scrooge,* she and Denise had decided to take a break. Denise planned her wedding, Lindsay helped finish up the renovations of the theater and concentrated on her notes for summarizing the good and bad points about the play.

Now that Denise and her brother Ethan were busy nesting and getting settled into married life, Lindsay was feeling like it was time to begin again.

But—begin what? That was the question. A serious drama? A comedy? A musical?

Thinking of the patrons, and the response she got from them, she was pretty sure something catchy and romantic was the ticket.

She needed to put on a play that would at the very least bring out the kind of crowds that *Scrooge* did. And, of course, there was the whole thing with ghosts. Should she ignore Sally McGraw, the rumored resident ghost, completely? Put on a mystery like she and Denise had planned?

As she thought of Sally, Lindsay's stomach tightened again. Though she'd never actually *seen* the apparition, she'd felt her effects more than once.

Agatha Christie's *Ten Little Indians*? Maybe.

Maybe something that had to do with ghosts . . . *The Ghost and Mrs. Muir*? She could have sworn she'd come across the stage production of that a few years ago. Maybe—

"Hey, look out!"

She turned to the voice just as a chunk of a two-by-four, or whatever it was, sailed toward her. Time seemed to go into slow motion as she craned her head to watch the board slowly fall from a second floor window toward her, spiraling like a javelin as it did. She scrambled to her left.

It wasn't quite far enough. The edge of the wood scraped her arm and thigh as it landed with a loud thud, the force making her fall to the sidewalk.

"Ack!" she cried out as the hot cement jarred her senses as well as her palms. The scrapes on her hands temporarily took the sting from her leg and arm, reverberating across her body. "Oh!" she said again before resting her cheek on the ground.

Honestly, when was she ever going to look where she was going instead of analyzing everything she'd done, was doing, and planned to do?

"Hey! You okay?" A voice called out from the distance.

Dazed, she lifted her head toward the sound of quick footsteps from one of the construction work-ers. As her vision cleared, she noticed he wore heavy, grungy work boots that laced to the top of his ankles. Lindsay would bet a dollar that torrential showers of wood could rain on those boots and his feet wouldn't feel a thing.

It felt only natural to direct her gaze upward.

His legs were bare in the July heat. Khaki shorts, a tool belt, and a faded blue T-shirt covered up the rest of his impressive self. Raising her head a little higher, she noticed that his blond hair was a little long and a little curly, and seemed to frame his face very well. His mother must have told him long ago to always wear blue, because those piercing blue eyes were surely his best feature.

In fact, he looked so much like an angel, standing in front of her, the sun blazing around him, she kind of forgot to breathe. Surely she was imagining things again? She rested her head on the sidewalk again.

The angel knelt down beside her.

Oh, he smelled good too. How had he managed that while working in the heat all day? Wasn't he supposed to be sweaty?

"Hey. Miss? Miss, are you okay?"

Miss? Well, at least he wasn't treating her like she was ancient. With shaky movements, she sat up, the world spinning as she did so. Deliberately, she closed her eyes, then opened them back up slowly. "Yes?"

Those blue eyes widened, giving her an up-close-and-personal look at his pupils, wide with worry. As if in a trance she leaned forward.

He leaned back, muttering something under his breath as he did so. "Look, I'm really sorry about all this." He reached out to touch her arm, then drew his hand back just as quickly. "Did you notice, by chance, that you were walking right through the mid-dle of a construction site?"

Construction site? The news, and his proximity, jarred her again. She shook her head no, wincing with the motion, before finally speaking. "No, I . . . I didn't notice."

Deep lines fell into worn creases around his eyes, the only sign—as far as she could tell—that he spent hours in the sun.

"I hope you'll be okay. You're bleeding from about five different places." His blue eyes narrowed. "You look pretty beat up."

"Thanks for the observation." As Lindsay examined her arm, she had to admit that it did look pretty bad. A scratch about three inches long was bleeding steadily and sending off little points of pain up to her elbow. The side of her left calf didn't look so hot, either. And, if the wetness on her cheek was any indication, she wasn't just sweating.

She was just about to inspect the dampness when she caught sight of her palms. Each one had a kaleidoscope of rocks and pebbles embedded in them, and were oozing as well. Yeah, she felt beat up.

"I'll be okay." Then, because he looked so worried, and she'd never had had any desire to be a shrinking violet, she added, "I hadn't planned on getting my picture taken today anyway."

Amusement and pure relief filled his features as he grasped her right elbow and helped her to her feet. "Here, let me give you a hand."

She was in no position to ignore it. "Thanks."

Lindsay tried not to notice that his hand felt very

nice around her arm. Tried not to notice that his grip was far more gentle than she would have expected. And cool. How did his hand manage to be so cool in the heat? "Thanks for coming over to check on me."

"It was the least I could do." He pointed to the house under construction behind them. "I'm really sorry about all this. When I asked Jack to toss a board down below, I should have told him to yell a warning."

Even to her ringing ears, Lindsay knew that was a precaution he shouldn't have had to take. "Why? To warn all the trespassers?"

He chuckled. "At least to all pretty brunettes."

His words clicked in and sent a little tingle of awareness through her that had nothing to do with pain and everything to do with him. Her savior was extremely attractive.

Standing a full six inches taller than her five-foot-seven frame, his proximity made her feel feminine and attractive. It also was impossible to ignore that he seemed to be made of solid muscle. And . . . the warmth of his gaze betrayed that he seemed to be just as aware of her.

Lindsay tried not to feel a little burst of feminine satisfaction when her construction-worker-angel did a once-over of her figure and looked as if he hadn't found a thing wanting.

But then, just as quickly, their connection was over. He dropped his hand.

"Craig, she okay?" A guy standing in front of the site called out.

"You okay?" he asked dutifully, a touch of a smile reaching his mouth.

"I am."

"Yep!" he called back, finishing up their circular conversation.

The exchange made her chuckle. The warm tension between them made her keep talking, anything to prevent her from leaving right that minute. "I'm sorry, again. I was just thinking about work and I guess I wasn't paying attention. Thanks for coming over."

"No problem."

When he looked as if he was about to turn away, Lindsay stuck out her hand. "I'm Lindsay. Lindsay Flynn."

He clasped her fingers. "Craig Bennett."

"Nice to meet you."

He flashed a smile just as his fingers loosened their gentle grip. Their hands dropped.

Her pulse leaped. There was something about Craig Bennett that made her want to stand closer to him, clutch his hand again, catch his scent. "Um, what are you working on?"

"A tear-down re-do."

Thinking of the theater, she said, "I know all about those."

He turned from the construction sight to her once again. "Yeah? I can't picture you in construction."

"No, I'd be dangerous with a hammer. And I don't have the boots, either."

Pulling out a worn bandana from his back pocket, he dabbed at the line of blood on her arm. "If you have this much trouble around a worksite, I'd say we better keep you far, far away from all power tools."

Her arm stung, there was no doubt about it. So how come all she could feel was the touch of his fingertips through the soft fabric?

"The reason I know about re-do's is because I manage the Payton Theater. I was around last year when my brother Ethan was working on it."

"Ethan Flynn?"

"Yeah. Do you know him?"

"Only from my visits to his hardware store . . . and by reputation. He does good work."

"I'll pass on the compliment."

"Bennett?" Another guy called out. "You still on the clock?"

"Yeah. Hold on." Craig gestured to the work site. "I better get going. Glad you're okay."

"Thanks." She glanced at his bandana, now stained. "I'll wash this and bring it back to you."

"Don't worry about it."

A skitter of warmth flowed through her. She tamped it down when it occurred to her just how silly she was being. Grown women did not get excited about old bandanas as gifts.

She really needed to get out more.

Craig was still standing next to her, watching her dab at her cuts. Clearing her throat, she murmured, "Well. I better go get cleaned up."

"Probably a good idea." He stepped away. "Have you had a tetanus shot lately?"

"I don't know."

"You might check on that."

"Yet another bit of info I'd need to know if I was a construction worker?"

"Yep."

She laughed. "Well, I guess you can go to sleep to-night knowing that you did a good deed."

A slow smile lit his face. "I'll think of you when I close my eyes."

Lord have mercy. Lindsay was afraid she'd be thinking of him, too, but her thoughts would have more to do with his golden curly hair, blue eyes, and tanned torso. She struggled to keep their conversation casual. "If you hadn't called out to me, I could have gotten a good whack from that board."

"I'm glad you're not hurt any worse."

She was too. Though . . . why hadn't she been thinking that at the moment? And why was she suddenly glad she'd had an up-close-and-personal relationship with a two-by-four? "Well, thanks again, Craig. I promise next time I walk by I'll stay clear of the tape."

"Don't stay too far away, I'll want to see you." His eyes widened as his verbal slip hung in the air. "I mean, I'll want to see how you're doing."

As she met his gaze again, she felt yet another zing of awareness. There was something between the two of them—something more than just concern about her injuries or his work site.

Their connection was broken by yet another call from the work site. "Bennett? You coming or quitting?"

He waved a hand in their direction, causing another round of laughter and cat calls. "I better go."

"You should. I'd hate to be responsible for your unemployment."

"Don't worry about that. They're just . . ." His voice drifted off as he seemed to be at a loss of words. "Crazy."

She stepped away, then winced as the scrapes stung more than she'd anticipated. "Well. Bye."

"Bye."

Turning, she walked away, hearing him do the same.

She hadn't stepped more than a few more feet when she heard him again.

"Go to the doctor," he called out just before he crossed the taped line and trotted back to the site.

Just to make him smile, she waved a hand at him in just the way he had to the other workers. Picking up her purse, she hobbled down the sidewalk again.

Gosh, her cuts hurt.

Well, that would teach her, now wouldn't it? Walking into the middle of a construction site. But, honestly, wasn't that Craig Bennett cute?

He was a real guy's guy. Masculine. Attractive.

One look at Craig had assured her that his muscles came from hard work, not machines in a health club. His tan, from hours in the hot sun.

He didn't look like the type to easily put on a suit or to spend a lot of money on useless knickknacks. All of those characteristics appealed to her. What made her reaction that much more surprising was that she'd never figured she was the type of girl to even care about those types of traits.

Lindsay was just wondering if her brother's whirlwind romance had happened as unexpectedly as her little episode with Craig when she rounded the corner and just about barreled into Joanne Sawyer.

Obviously, it was time to start watching where she was going.

Joanne stopped in midstride and gasped. "Lindsay, you're bleeding! What happened to you?"

"Just a little run-in with a flying board," she said. "Ouch."

"Ouch is right." Lindsay shared a laugh with her.

She and Joanne were now distantly related. Lindsay's brother Ethan was married to Joanne's sister. From the moment they'd met, Lindsay knew she'd found a kindred spirit. Joanne was fun and adventurous, and always busy.

At the moment, she was also very pregnant. "How are you feeling?" Lindsay asked, glancing to Joanne's bulging belly.

"Whale-like."

"It's almost over, right?"

"Kind of. Stratton and I are expecting Junior to be born the end of September."

"For what it's worth, you don't look like a whale. You look very pretty." Joanne was wearing a jean jumper, a white T-shirt, and Keds. She looked trim and fit and very, very happy.

"I know I look better than you. What happened exactly?"

Lindsay shrugged, the movement making her wince. "I was walking along Elm, not paying attention to anything around me when all of the sudden a guy yells out from that house they're redoing, 'Look out!' Next thing I know, I'm trying to dodge flying objects." She laughed as she recalled how that board had looked sailing toward her in slow-motion. "Just call me Chicken Little."

"Come on, you're coming with me to see Stratton."

Since Joanne's husband was a doctor, and now that

all thoughts of Craig Bennett were fading in conjunction with the growing pain flowing through her right side, she agreed.

Amazing what weird things could happen when you least expect it.

Chapter Two

"You want to go to the Grill for a beer when we get off?" Jack asked after chugging a full bottle of water in one gulp. "It's hot as sin out here."

Though cooling off did sound great, Craig shook his head. "Not tonight. I've got to go see my nephew Brandon for a little while."

"Oh, yeah. How's he doing?"

"He's out of the hospital, but other than that, not so well. Having pneumonia in the middle of the summer is pretty much a bummer all around. I'm going to bring him a couple of videos and hang out for a while. My sister's husband, Jerry, is out of town again and she's going crazy."

"Last night you were helping your mother paint her kitchen."

"It was her bathroom. And yeah, I know."

"A couple of days ago you were visiting your sister Lauren at the university."

Craig laughed at the way Jack said "university," like Lauren was going to Harvard, instead of a nearby community college. "Lauren was sure she had a rat the size of Miami in her apartment."

Jack raised an eyebrow. "There was no one else around to check it out?"

There hadn't been. Lauren had been waiting for him in the parking lot and had hugged him tightly when he had, indeed, found a big ol' nasty mouse in the trap they'd set a week before. "Lauren's my baby sister. She doesn't need to deal with rodents." Wondering what the sudden inquisition was all about, Craig asked, "What's going on?"

"Too much. You're working fifty hours a week. Sometimes more."

Craig still didn't know what Jack was trying to get at. "So? You are too."

"Yeah, but I still have time to go to the Grill after work. I'm not running around trying to take care of the world in my time off."

"Just your wife and kid." Embarrassed that Jack was making such a big deal out of his obligations, he chided, "What are you, my mother?"

"Nah. It's just . . . you ought to learn how to relax, Craig."

"What? Start blocking in 'me' time?"

Jack's cheeks flushed. "Maybe. I don't know."

"You sound like you've been reading women's magazines." Glancing at his digital watch, Craig stepped another two steps back. "Sorry—I gotta go. See you tomorrow." Before Jack could refer to one more thing that he'd been doing, Craig walked off the site and down the sidewalk.

He preferred walking to work on most days. It gave him some time to decompress, and actually saved time, since the July sun made his black Ford F150 feel like a furnace for the first ten minutes. By the time it had gotten cool enough to sit down, he could be halfway home.

Speaking of walking, Craig couldn't help but smile as he passed the exact spot where Lindsay was foolish enough to get caught by the flying board. What a gal. What a *woman*. He corrected himself, now that his little nieces—all of six years old—were on a feminist kick.

Long brownish blonde hair. The type of slim, lanky build that showed she wasn't into frills or high heels. Natural. She was the type of woman he'd always been attracted to. She looked like she wouldn't mind if he occasionally had dirt under his fingernails or stains on his jeans. She looked like she wouldn't have any problem catching a movie or a burger at the Grill.

He'd felt something between them when they'd talked. An awareness that had sprung up and caught him by the collar. He hadn't dabbed her arm just because she was bleeding.

No, he'd wanted to touch her, which was completely crazy. She probably hadn't thought about him for more than two seconds. Shoot, she was probably already listing in her mind the hundred ways she did not ever want to walk near a building site again.

Which meant he'd probably never see her again.

Not that he was looking for a date. No, as Jack had pointed out, he had his hands full with family commitments. He was the go-to uncle when his siblings needed a much-needed break from parenting. He was the Mr. Fix-it guy for his mom, since no one else seemed to be able to hold a screwdriver. He was everything they needed him to be, and he knew it. That's what being the oldest got you—being raised to be responsible.

Yeah, he was an easy target. He knew it. They knew it. He couldn't say no.

And though he didn't even want to admit it to himself, more than once he wished he did have some time to do something else. Anything that didn't involve paychecks or obligations.

His wishes brought back a vow he'd made three years before, when he'd been lucky enough to walk away from a car accident. He'd promised himself that he'd spend more time enjoying life, not just getting through it.

Funny how it had taken another accident to remind him he wasn't doing a very good job about following through.

"Being sick in the summer is so lame," Brandon said after Craig handed him a couple of movies he'd rented.

"I completely agree," Craig said, pulling up a chair beside his nephew. As nonchalantly as he could, he examined the kid. He didn't look too good. His color was off and he had circles under his eyes.

"All my friends are either playing sports or going to the water parks."

The complaint made Craig smile. "You must be feeling better. A week ago I don't think you would've cared."

Brandon shrugged. "A week ago I was in the hospital." With a frown he added, "Again."

"What did Dr. Sawyer say about that?"

"He said that I tried to do too much too quickly."

"Maybe you did."

"I guess." Brandon glanced at his door. "Mom's had to take a bunch of time off work."

"I heard that. She's got a good boss, though. He knows what's important: for her to take care of you." Mentally Craig made a note to remember to give

Leah some money when he left. Her cut-down work hours, together with the hospital bills, were probably making things financially tight.

"Yeah, but I heard her and Dad talking about bills the other night." Brandon bent his head down, looking for once like a regular ten-year-old instead of far older. "I feel like it's all my fault."

"It's not. No one wants to have pneumonia."

"But—"

Craig stilled the next comment with a hand. "Let me tell you something. You could worry all night about why you got sick . . . about how come it's lasting so long. How much the bills are, how your mom's missing work . . . but it wouldn't solve anything. All you need to do is worry about getting better. Your parents will worry about everything else."

"What if I get sick again?"

"Then *I'm* going to be really worried, and so will the rest of the family." Attempting to lighten things up, Craig added, "And then we're all going to have to go back to Children's and visit you again. It would really tick me off, too, since I've got a big date this weekend."

Brandon rolled his eyes. "Uncle Craig, you never have dates."

No, he didn't. "I should, though. I'm going to start dating all the time, so get well, okay?"

"Okay. I get it."

"Get what?" Leah, Brandon's mom said from the doorway.

Brandon glanced at Craig, as if begging him silently to not divulge their talk. "Nothing. Just guy stuff."

Leah looked relieved. "Oh, good. I was going to tell you that I made enough food for an army. Stay for dinner, would you? With Jerry gone so much, Brandon and I get tired of each other's company."

In a split second, the privacy—and the opportunity to put his feet up and watch a mindless hour of TV—floated right by. "Sure. I'd love to," he said.

Chapter Three

Lindsay loved the old theater building. She loved the way the old wood smelled, especially since it had been waxed and sanded and shined until it glistened.

She liked the way the antique fixtures made her think about what life had been like in the 1930s, when crowds of people came to see grand musicals and reviews. The ornately carved columns and intricately carved wood around the doorways were the original pieces that were described in the *Payton Registrar's* historical papers.

Lindsay loved that she was now a part of the theater, and its future. One day someone would be perusing old crumbly copies of the *Payton Registrar* and read about Lindsay Flynn's productions. Lindsay hoped her accomplishments would be notewor-thy . . . and inspire a smile or two.

Yes, things at the Sally McGraw Theater were go-ing well; she just wished she had a better handle on the strange happenings around the place.

Denise seemed to think it could all be attributed to Sally, the theater's namesake.

Lindsay kind of hoped it was, otherwise there was someone around the place who was inordinately fond of big band music, talcum powder, and open windows.

Gosh, it seemed as if every single time she was just getting comfortable, when she was just settling into a good book or a television show, or hard at work fine-tuning a script or set design, a blasted boom box would click on and scare her half to death.

"I don't know if I can take much more of her shenanigans, Denise," Lindsay admitted after they'd gone through two hours of play selections and day-to-day work, only to be interrupted by a slam and the faint sound of the Tommy Dorsey Orchestra billow-ing out.

As she turned toward the noise, Denise grinned. "I don't think Sally means to scare you. She's just do-ing her own thing."

"I don't think Sally has a 'routine' to do. I think she just lies in wait for me, counting the hours and waiting for the perfect opportunity to make her appearance known and freak me out."

"Oh, Lindsay. Don't you think you're getting a little too uptight about all this?"

"Hmm. Let me see . . . No. Just the other day I was watching old reruns of *Happy Days* when she turned on every light on the first floor. I was shaking so bad I had to clutch the banister of the staircase when I went down to set everything right." A little shiver curved down Lindsay's spine as she remembered just how shaken she'd been . . . and annoyed with herself for letting her imagination get the best of her.

Denise looked pointedly at Lindsay's stitches. "With your track record, you need to grab hold of everything you possibly can."

"Ha-ha. All I'm saying is that living here has its challenges."

"I would agree. It *is* hard to live on the top floor of a theater."

"No, it's hard to live in the same building as a restless ghost with a bone to pick."

Denise frowned. "A bone to pick? Do you think she's unhappy?"

"I'm not sure. Sometimes I get the feeling that she wants something to be done." Then, listening to her own words, Lindsay shook her head. "Would you listen to us? We're psychoanalyzing a ghost!"

Laughing, Denise shook her head. "I guess it does seem pretty far-fetched. Um . . . are you trying to tell me in a roundabout way that you want to move out of here?"

Lindsay thought for a long moment before replying. Was she unhappy? Was she scared to death? No, it was more that she just wanted someone to vent to. She told Denise as much.

Visibly relieved, Denise smiled. "I'm so glad. I can't tell you how happy I am that someone is living here. It's nice to know you're looking out for the place." Running a hand along a neatly patched wall, she added, "This building had so many problems when we were fixing it up, I was really worried there were going to be problems long into the future. With you here, I know that any major problems won't go unnoticed."

Thinking back to her conversation with Craig about tools and construction, Lindsay said, "I wouldn't put much stock in my knowledge."

"I'm not," Denise said honestly. "But I do think you'll notice if a pipe bursts."

"Your belief in me is endearing."

"I believe you spend the majority of your time in the clouds," she retorted. "I'm glad you do. I think that's why you're so good at directing plays."

"Thanks, I think."

"Oh, hush. I'm just saying we're glad you're here. Ethan's said as much too."

Since Ethan was her brother and also Denise's husband, Lindsay didn't say a word, though she knew he was very glad he wasn't stuck living on the top floor of a historic theater. Ethan fit far better in his cozy townhouse near the river.

"How is Ethan, by the way? I haven't seen him lately."

"Busy. The hardware store is crazy busy right now. And he's got two papers to write for his college course. I've been working the counter and trying to keep his remodeling jobs organized."

Lindsay knew that while many people thought of soft-spoken Denise simply as Ethan's wife, she was much more than that. She was his true partner in every sense of the word. Denise had a gift for organization and dealing with people that was admirable. In addition, her steadfast love for her husband allowed Ethan to feel confident enough to expand his carpentry business. "You sure are good for him."

"He's good for me," Denise corrected. "I'm so thankful I met him. I had never felt connected to my family or the town until I met Ethan." Leaning back in her chair, she mused, "Isn't it funny that it took a stranger to make me feel close to my family?"

Thinking back to how a relative stranger had just

made a huge impact on herself, Lindsay nodded. "Maybe not so funny. He is a good guy."

"Yeah. And he's so cute."

"I don't want to hear he's cute," Lindsay teased. "He's my brother!"

Narrowing her eyes, Denise asked, "What about you?"

"What about me?"

"You and love. Have you met any interesting men lately?"

Shaggy blond hair, a pair of biceps practically molded of steel, and piercing blue eyes taunted her. So did the likelihood that she and a certain sexy construction worker would never cross paths again. "No."

"You waited just a minute too long to be believable. Come on, 'fess up. Who is it?"

How could Lindsay admit that she'd fallen for a guy she'd almost literally "fallen" into? "There's nobody. You know I don't have time for that, anyway."

"Sure you do. Everyone has time for love."

"You're speaking like a true romantic." Flipping through the papers in front of her, Lindsay added, "We both know that's not me."

"Maybe, maybe not." Pointing to the white bandage on Lindsay's arm, Denise was filled with concern. "How are you feeling, by the way?"

"All right."

"Did you have to get many stitches?"

"Six. I could have probably done without them, but Stratton said if I didn't, I'd have a sizable scar on my arm. He also was kind enough to gift me with a nasty tetanus shot."

"Good." Denise shook her head. "What a freak accident that was."

"It was freaky." So had been the instant connection she'd felt with Craig. She'd been so caught up in him she'd hardly felt any pain . . . only the rush of pleasure she felt when he'd helped her to her feet. And that had been embarrassing.

Rummaging through the stack of scripts that littered the table, Lindsay attempted to move on. "That accident is gone and forgotten. I'm glad too. I've got just about all I can handle with this theater."

Worry lines deepened around Denise's eyes. "You know, when I hired you to manage the theater, I never thought that it would take over your life."

"It hasn't."

"It might be." She tapped her pencil. "It sounds like it is. I don't see you do much except work on the plays, decorating the theater, or organizing the crazy files up in the attic."

"It's all part of the job that you hired me to do."

"Please take some time for yourself."

"I am."

"If you need some help, promise you'll let me know."

She would never say it, but Lindsay knew she would never ask Denise to do more than she was already doing. When Denise had hired her to manage the theater, she'd made a hundred dreams of Lindsay's come to life. There was no way she was willing to either disappoint Denise . . . or embarrass Ethan by not giving the theater a hundred percent.

"I don't need help . . . well, beyond giving me the okay to begin production on a new play," she said with a bright smile. "So, boss, what do you think? *Arsenic and Old Lace* or *The Ghost and Mrs. Muir*?"

"*The Ghost and Mrs. Muir,* of course. I can't wait to see what you can do with a crabby seafaring ghost."

"I am looking forward to the challenge, myself. Ever see the movie with Gene Tierney and Rex Harrison?"

"Of course. Only about a hundred times."

Lindsay pulled out a calendar. "It's now the end of July. I was thinking we could plan for the first week in October."

"Whatever you want. Just let me know what you need."

"I'll need to do some thinking, then meet with you in two weeks to iron out a budget."

Denise jotted down some notes. "I'll look forward to that."

Lindsay laughed. "You hate budgets."

"I'm getting better at them." She stood up to leave. "Speaking of things to do, I promised Ethan I'd go let out Comet before I head into the store. Thanks for meeting me so early."

"No problem."

Denise turned to her right as the boom box kicked on again. "And don't worry so much. Everything around here is going to be just fine. The Payton community is going to love *Ghost*."

Denise laughed. "I know, I know. If the ghost is happy, we're all happy. See you later. And relax!"

As Lindsay watched her leave, she knew that relaxation was the last thing she'd be doing. With a new play to produce, she had a script to finalize, ideas for sets and costumes to organize, and budgets to work over.

Shaking her head about it all, Lindsay did what she did best: work.

With multiple calendars in front of her, as well as her laptop and various stage productions of *The Ghost and Mrs. Muir,* she set about organizing the perfect setup for the Sally McGraw Theater.

Before she knew it, two hours had passed, then three. When her stomach started growling, she knew it was time to take a break. It was just as well that there was nothing in her refrigerator upstairs; she needed to get out into the sunshine and take a break.

The Grill was sure to have an endless supply of

fresh salads and cheeseburgers. After putting everything in neat piles and warning Sally to keep her
paws off of them, she headed out again.

The July sun was in all of its glory, making the
air hot enough to yearn for iced tea, and humid
enough to yearn for air-conditioning. As she passed
the construction site, she couldn't help but glance
up at the guys hammering and sawing, and doing
whatever else construction guys did, all with a
boom box playing old seventies' and eighties' music and a hefty amount of good-natured ribbing and
laughing.

Lindsay couldn't help but slow her steps. The guys
were gorgeous. At least half of them had their shirts
off, with ripped abs and finely honed pectorals
proudly displayed. She couldn't help but admire how
they walked along planks of wood with a confidence
and poise that people in few other occupations could
possess.

Then, just as she was going to turn away and concentrate on food, she spied Craig. She swallowed
hard as she noticed he, too, had his shirt off.

His skin was coppery and smooth. The barest
brush of hair covered his chest and made a beeline
down his stomach. Baggy cargo shorts were cinched
to his waist with a worn leather tool belt.

The humidity loved his hair. A riot of curls

brushed his cheeks and neck, once again drawing her eye to his bare chest and shoulders.

Blue eyes spotted her too. "Hey!" he called down from his perch near a second story window.

Craig's shout made Lindsay's whole world slow down. Hammers stopped pounding in midair, music faded to a faint murmur, and every construction worker turned to look at her.

Lindsay held up a hand to wave, but he was already climbing down the stairs. "Hi," he said when he reached the main floor.

"Hi."

He rubbed a hand along his left bicep. "How's your arm?"

Not nearly as great as his! "Better."

"Did you need stitches?"

"Yep. A shot too." She felt her cheeks heat as the whole crew checked her out. Someone blew out a wolf whistle, though Lindsay sensed it was howled in fun, mainly to tease Craig—not out of disrespect to her.

"Go on out there, Bennett, if you're going to get all chatty," one of the guys muttered.

After giving the speaker a rude gesture, Craig trotted forward. "Don't go anywhere, Linds," he called out, easily stepping over a pile of discarded boards.

Her feet were so planted, Lindsay knew she wasn't

going to be able to take a step on her own. Motionless, she watched Craig pull out a faded bandana from a cargo pocket and wipe his hands and neck hastily.

Lindsay tried not to groan as her pulse speeded up in direct conjunction with his approach.

As he loped closer, more guys whistled and yelled out catcalls. He gestured to them again, right before he treated her to a beautiful, genuine smile. "I was wondering if you were ever going to walk by here again."

Her gaze skimmed across his bare chest. Muscular and finely honed, it looked even better up close than from a distance. Resolutely, she pulled her eyes upward. "It's hard not to pass by. Elm is in the middle of the downtown."

"Really? Did you walk by here yesterday? The day before?"

"No." Had he been looking for her? The thought made her both uncomfortable and curiously happy. "I actually took another route yesterday." She shrugged. "I was pretty embarrassed about my little accident . . ." Her voice drifted off. What could she add? That while she'd been mortified, she'd also been sure that they might never have a reason to talk again? Afraid she'd merely imagined his attraction?

Craig blinked. "And?"

"Oh, nothing. I was just being silly." Clearing her

throat, she added, "I was just on my way to the Grill to have some lunch."

He glanced at his watch. "It's three."

She tried to make a joke about her crazy eating habits. "Three o'clock is always the best time for lunch. The restaurants are hardly crowded."

"I bet not."

"I guess you've been up for hours, huh?"

"Since five this morning."

"My day started a little bit later." She shrugged. "I usually don't get out of bed until ten." Struggling to keep the conversation going, she blurted, "I'm a night owl."

"Oh, yeah?" A spark of humor lit his eyes as she yearned to close her own in frustration.

Had she really just used a childish phrase to describe herself to the most gorgeous man she'd ever seen? No wonder she practically lived in a dream world! Hoping to reestablish herself as an independent woman, she said, "I've been working today, reading scripts. The time got away from me."

"You want some company?"

"Excuse me?"

"Company for lunch?" He gestured to the site. "I'm due for a break."

Lindsay knew she had no business pursuing a relationship with Craig. But self-preservation kicked in. "I'd love the company," she said, her words bursting forth like she'd swallowed a healthy dose of truth serum.

Craig and his white teeth treated her to a very masculine grin. "Good." With economical moves, he unfastened his tool belt, which unfortunately drew her eyes back to his amazing physique, which in turn made her realize she'd been staring at him like he was lunch.

If he noticed her hungry stare, he didn't say so. "I'll meet you there in ten minutes." Nodding to an older man who was watching them with his arms crossed, Craig said, "I've just got to go tell the foreman I'm taking a little lunch break."

"I'll, uh, save you a seat."

With a smile, he turned away, already walking nimbly over the scattered pieces of wood and trash.

Lindsay walked to the Grill, wondering what in the world she was doing.

"Lindsay's over there," Sam Ravel said as Craig entered the restaurant.

Craig murmured his thanks as his eyes did their best to adjust to the cool, darker surroundings. A blast of cool air from a window unit fanned his face as he passed the bar area and finally came toward Lindsay.

Craig approached her table and couldn't help but

grin as he noticed Sam and a couple of the waiters give him a double take.

Not that he could blame them. Even to his eyes, he and Lindsay seemed a pretty crazy pairing. He'd done some checking on Lindsay Flynn since her near miss with his flying two-by-four.

Her brother Ethan, owner of the hardware store, always had a story to tell about his kid sister. She liked sports, talked too much and too fast, had tunnel vision when it came to work . . .

Ethan was a good guy. At least once a week someone from the crew ran in there to pick up emergency supplies. He did good finishing work too. Craig knew a couple of guys who'd done some work in the theater when Ethan was renovating it. Everyone had been surprised and impressed with the quality of the job.

Craig would never have thought that Ethan would have a sister who was so different from him. While he was quiet and easygoing, the word was she was quick-witted and hyper.

All he knew was that she was pretty in the way he liked. Slim and long-legged. Long ash-colored hair that he'd only seen tied back in a ponytail. Pretty brown eyes that curved up a little in the corners.

And today, she was dressed for the hot weather in white shorts and a black cotton halter top. Her lightly tanned shoulders drew his eye like little else could.

So did the way he'd noticed her looking at him. For the first time in a long while, nothing in his life mattered but being with her.

"I saved you a spot," she said brightly as he pulled out his chair.

"Thanks."

"I didn't know what you wanted to drink, so I just ordered you a water. They'll give you something else, too, if you just ask."

"Thanks for the tip," he murmured, wondering why she was talking so fast . . . and so much. Was she nervous for some reason?

"Sorry. Of course you know that." She fiddled with her menu. "I can't decide what to eat. My head is saying salad, but my stomach is thinking about a cheeseburger and fries."

"I'm going for the burger myself."

"I bet you are, I mean you've been up since five, working outside." Lindsay's brown eyes shot to his chest, then darted back to the menu. "Hmm. I guess I should try a salad. I mean, I think we're supposed to have four helpings of fruits and vegetables a day, right?"

He had no idea what she was talking about, but he vaguely remembered doing cut-out paper collages of food groups back in third grade.

Just to see what she would do, he said, "I usually get five or six helpings a day."

Her fingers drummed the table. "I've tried to drink vegetable juice, but I never did like that stuff."

Vegetable juice sounded nasty. "What *do* you like, Lindsay?"

"Milkshakes. French fries."

"Me too." He pushed his menu aside. He was so captivated by her, Craig knew the server could put a bottle of vegetable juice and a salad in front of him and he'd think it tasted good. "What else do you like?"

Her eyes widened at the question, and to his surprise, she even waited a few moments before answering, taking the time to give the query some thought. "I like working. I like the theater."

Slightly disappointed by the lack of information, he probed some more, eager to know more about her. "What do you do for fun? You know, when you go out on dates. Movies? Dancing?"

She chuckled. "I guess. Truthfully, I haven't had much time to go out lately. Work consumes me."

Family consumed him, but although it was by choice, he'd been suddenly looking forward to doing other things as well. "Too bad, huh?"

"I guess. Actually, running this theater has been a dream of mine for too long to not spend a hundred percent of my time on it now. I don't have time for love or romance."

He couldn't help but laugh at that. "Nobody *doesn't* have time for those things. They're a part of life."

"Not this life. At least, not right now."

Luckily, their burgers came before he could comment on that, or consider why he cared.

Craig bit into his with relish, realizing that he hadn't eaten in a good seven hours. Not since a hastily grabbed apple on his way out the door early that morning.

By the looks of things, Lindsay was happy to be eating the burger as well. She bit into her food with relish, as if she hadn't eaten in days. For a brief moment he was struck by how she wasn't overtly flirting with him, hinting about dining together again.

Craig didn't know whether to be disappointed or curiously pleased.

Lindsay was so different than his last girlfriend. Pam had doted on him. Every day when he'd come off a job, he'd find multiple messages on his cell phone, on his home phone, asking when he was going to get off, seeing if he wanted to come over for dinner, telling him about plans she made. After the novelty of having a woman waiting on him had worn off, he had found Pam's possessiveness irritating.

He'd broken off with her a few months ago, and heard that she was now dating a guy from the bank.

The first time he saw them together, he'd felt a stab of remorse. He'd hated the feeling, and hated that he'd missed her attention more than he'd missed her. Craig didn't like to think that he was so self-centered.

"Earth to Craig."

Quickly, he shook his head. "Sorry. My mind drifted. I guess the fat and grease affected my brain for a few minutes."

"I wouldn't say that too loud. They're pretty proud of their burgers here."

He chuckled, popping a french fry in his mouth as he scanned her bare shoulders. Her skin was rich and supple, drawing his eyes to every bare inch of it. An unfamiliar spark of desire ran through him, and Craig knew he had to see this girl again—as soon as possible.

Surely she hadn't been serious when she talked about being too busy for love and romance?

"So, if I asked you out, what would you say?"

Her eyes widened. After a few seconds, she shook her head. "I'd say thanks, but not right now."

Her rejection hit his pride in the gut, hard. Struggling hard to play it cool, he laughed it off. "Wow. You really know how to make a guy feel good."

Relief filled her eyes as she laughed too. It drew his attention back to her smile and to the way her eyes lit up, like she had an inner glow. Of course, that made him want to be with her even more.

"It's nothing personal," she murmured. "It's just like I said—I really don't have time for dating."

"But if you did? What would you say then?"

A pretty pink sheen brushed over her cheeks. "Then I'd say yes."

There was no way he was going to let her get away from him now. There was something between them, something electric. Something he'd never had with Pam, no matter how hard they'd tried. "We'll just have to come up with a way for you to have more time."

"That's not possible."

"Not possible?" In Craig's book, everything was possible. Take him walking away from that car accident. That episode alone convinced him that anything could happen.

Struggling to keep his words light, he said, "These people you work for must be tough."

"Hardly. Ethan is married to the owner."

Now nothing made sense. He'd do just about anything for his sisters, and they'd used it to their advantage all their lives. Ethan Flynn didn't seem that different from himself. "Your own brother won't let you take any time off?"

"Oh, he would. They both would. But, I don't want to let them down," she explained, pushing her dish away. "Asking me to manage the theater was a real risk on their part."

"Why was it so risky?"

"I'd been living in the city, trying to make a name for myself. Nothing was happening."

"You're young. How long did you try?"

"Long enough to get more than a couple of doors

slammed in my face. When Ethan called and said I could talk to Denise about managing the theater, it felt so perfect. And it has been. I love it. I love living near my brother too." She sipped her Coke. "Craig, I'm really glad we got to eat together, and I appreciate how nice you've been to me, especially since I was in your work site and made such a mess of things."

"Well, then—"

"But I'm not ready for anything more," she continued. "I can't afford to have a personal life, not when everything I've ever wanted professionally is in my grasp. I'm about to produce another play. If I make it a success, then Denise will really be glad she hired me."

"And then you'll be free to date?"

"Maybe." She shrugged. "Of course, if it does well, I want to see if Denise will let me try out a new play, something a little different or not as familiar." Leaning forward, she said, "I'd love to have our playhouse be known as someplace where people could go to see up-and-coming playwrights."

"Putting on plays sounds impressive, but I have a feeling it wouldn't hold a candle to having a real life."

"Craig—"

The waitress came to take their plates before she could complete her thought, which was probably just as well. He was disappointed and irritated. And irritated that he was disappointed. After all, he didn't really know Lindsay Flynn. He just thought she was attractive. There were plenty of other women in the world who were good-looking, right?

Wrong. Craig knew it hadn't just been her looks that had sparked his interest. But as memories of the way Pam had clung to him sank in, he grabbed the check that their server had left on the table. The last thing he wanted to do was cling to Lindsay like Pam had clung to him. "I'm glad we had lunch together, but I better head on back. I'll see you around."

She looked surprised at his abrupt departure. "Are you mad?"

"Not at all," he lied, knowing good and well that he had no business being upset. "I just need to get back to work."

She stilled him with a hand. "Wait a minute. You took the bill."

He waved it. "I know."

"But I didn't want you to pay for me. I mean this wasn't a date or anything."

Her refusal to even acknowledge something so simple ticked him off. "How about we just call it my treat for hitting you with a board?" he asked, trying to keep their conversation light.

"But it was my fault."

"It's just a burger. Don't worry. See ya," he called

out before she could tell him again how she wasn't interested in dating.

He didn't want to hear anymore about how busy she was. Craig was feeling foolish enough that his pride had been hurt.

Quickly, Craig paid at the front register, then went back to the site. As he approached, a couple of the guys whistled, ready to give him grief. He did his best to smile and act sheepish, though in truth, he was more than a little dismayed.

He was completely head over heels for Lindsay Flynn . . . and she could care less.

When Pamela found out, she was going to have a field day. It totally served him right.

Chapter Four

"We're so glad you could stop by," Daphne said to Lindsay when she arrived at the Reece house for dinner on Sunday evening. "None of my kids could make dinner tonight."

Since Mr. and Mrs. Reece had five kids and multiple grandchildren, Lindsay was a little taken aback. "It's just me?"

"Yes, won't that be nice? I thought we could have a little intimate dinner out on the back patio. Jim's cooking chicken."

Lindsay felt too skeptical to say much. Daphne Reece could give lessons to steamrollers. "Thank you."

"Tea?"

"Please." As Daphne walked toward the kitchen in her heeled sandals, Lindsay had the uncomfortable feeling that she'd just been set up. Sunday night dinners were a constant tradition in the Reece family. Ethan had both talked of them fondly, and with more than a little exasperation from time to time. Though it was unusual for all five children to show up with their spouses, Lindsay had never heard of all of them abandoning their parents.

And she'd never, ever heard of Daphne and Jim Reece inviting family friends over alone unless they had a reason. Quickly her mind ran through prospective scenarios. Since Daphne and Jim were on the board of the theater, they might have had a problem with how Lindsay had been operating it.

Gosh, maybe they wanted to fire her?

Panic set in. Did Denise have a problem and not feel as if she could talk to Lindsay about it, and so had enlisted her parents instead?

That didn't sound like Denise, but Denise was also kind of shy and probably was more than a little caught off guard by Lindsay's forthright attitude.

Or maybe the problem was with Ethan and Denise? Were things not going well in their marriage and Mr. and Mrs. Reece were worried? Frantically, Lindsay tried to recall the last time she'd seen the two together.

It had been at their townhouse a few evenings ago. Ethan had been studying for a college class he was taking, and Denise had cooked dinner. They'd held hands and kissed enough for Lindsay to clear her throat to remind them that she was still in the room.

No, Ethan and Denise couldn't be having marriage trouble.

"Here we are, Lindsay," Daphne said as she handed her an ornately painted china cup. "This is raspberry tea. What do you think?"

As she took a small sip, Lindsay was pleasantly surprised. "It's very good."

"I thought so too." Daphne sat down across from her and crossed her capri-covered legs. "So, how are you?"

"Oh, fine."

"Dear, I think we both know that's not true."

Sheer panic bolted through Lindsay as she tried to guess what *wasn't* fine. "The theater's—"

"I'm not talking about the theater."

She guessed again. "Ethan and Denise—"

"Are better than good," Daphne easily interrupted. "They act just like newlyweds. Of course, they are newlyweds. Jim and I think they're adorable."

"A little too adorable, in my opinion," Jim Reece added as he walked out to the patio, a plate of marinated chicken in his hands. "The other night I stopped by their place and they acted like they could hardly wait for me to leave." As Jim set his dish down, his expression softened. "Hello, Lindsay. Glad you could come over."

Lindsay started to stand up. "Mr. Reece."

Daphne stilled her with a hand. "Sit down, dear. Jim and I've been talking. We want you to know that we're really glad we're all friends."

"I am too."

"We'd love to be here for you if you need us, especially since your parents are so far away."

Her parents were three hours north, but at the moment, that seemed beside the point. "Thank you."

"Yes. We're here for you if you need anything. Anything at all." Patting Lindsay's hand, she added, "We don't want you to worry another minute."

"Not another minute," Jim echoed.

Anything? Another minute? Lindsay bit her lip as she tried once again to guess what the Reeces were talking about. What had she done? "Thank you?"

"You're welcome."

"How's the arm?" Jim asked. "When do you get your stitches out?"

"Next week."

Jim pointed to her scraped-up leg, the red marks and scratches blazing a trail along her calf. "And your leg?"

"It's better too."

"Your hands and cheek?"

Lindsay held up two hands. "Fine."

Mrs. Reece nodded. "Good. Joanne called me as soon as you left Stratton's office. Really, Lindsay, I just don't know what Payton is coming to, if we have to practically look up at the sky as we're walking to search for flying objects."

"I don't think the town at large is going to have to do that, just me. The accident was purely my fault."

"Are you sure? Why, I almost visited those construction workers and gave them a piece of my mind."

The idea of Daphne Reece sashaying through a construction site was mind-boggling. "I hope you won't do that," she said in a rush. "It really was my fault. Craig couldn't have been more conciliatory."

Daphne carefully placed her tea cup back down on the table. "Craig? Who's Craig?"

"He's the construction worker who helped me."

"Well, that's nice that someone took the time to make sure you were okay."

"Oh, he did more than that. He rushed over while I was sitting there on the ground with the wind knocked out of me, and helped me up." Recalling just how attracted she'd been to him from the first instant, she added softly, "He really is very nice."

"What's this Craig's last name?"

"Bennett."

A new brightness entered Daphne's expression. "Craig Bennett. Well, well. I don't think I know him. Do you, Jim?"

"Nope." He flipped the chicken over and tapped

the tongs on the grill. "But if he practically saved your life, Lindsay, I'd say I need to buy him a beer."

"My life wasn't in danger, just my arm. And I've already thanked him. Many times. We went out to eat the other day."

"That sounds fun."

"It wasn't planned. It just . . . happened."

"Those are the best kinds of surprises."

Daphne's speculative glance made Lindsay more than a little uncomfortable. What was the purpose of this visit? "It wasn't a big deal." To emphasize her point, she added, "I doubt I'll ever see him again."

"He didn't like you?"

"No, I think he did. He asked me out."

"And you said no? He must not be attractive."

"No, he's very attractive."

"So, he's not nice?"

"He is. He's terrific. It's just that I'm very busy with the theater."

Jim put down his tongs. "How busy are you?"

"Very busy. Denise gave me the green light to start another production. I was thinking we'd put on *The Ghost and Mrs. Muir.*"

Easily sidetracked, Daphne smiled. "Oh, I've always loved that old movie."

"Me too. At first I was thinking *Arsenic and Old Lace,* but after careful consideration, Denise and I thought *The Ghost and Mrs. Muir* would be the best follow-up to *Scrooge.*"

"Yes, it would. I love how you're keeping the mystery theater idea. It goes perfectly with the rumors about it being haunted."

As Lindsay thought of her latest war with Sally, she couldn't help but agree.

"Now we just have to make sure you have time to go out with Craig."

"Oh—"

"We sure are glad you're adjusting so well to life in Payton."

"I . . . I am?"

As Daphne and Jim shared yet another knowing look, Lindsay sipped her tea. After a while, Daphne brought out a plate of twice-baked potatoes and a crisp green salad. Jim placed the chicken in front of them.

After a brief blessing, they began to eat in earnest. But nothing tasted good to Lindsay. She hated secrets, and she hated feeling that she was the cause of someone's stress or worry. Finally, when it seemed that all Daphne and Jim wanted to talk about was the weather, Lindsay broached the subject that they'd been skating around all evening. "What did you mean earlier, when you said you wanted to talk to me?"

"Oh, nothing. We were a little concerned that you were having a difficult time getting settled in Payton, but now that we've talked, it's obvious we had nothing to worry about."

After their talk? What had they talked about? "But—"

Jim cut her off. "Next Sunday we're going to the club for a pig roast. Have you ever been to one?"

"No."

"It's practically a Cincinnati tradition. Do say you'll come. The whole family will be there."

"I'll come."

"Good. There's always a good crowd. It will be fun."

Later, when Daphne was walking her to the door, Lindsay paused. "I thought I'd start casting the play in a month. Will that be okay with y'all?" she asked, since they were both on the Board of Directors.

"Of course, dear. You know we're only there as a formality, just in case Denise needs a helping hand." Patting her shoulder, she added, "Please try and relax some. Go out, make friends. Say yes to that Craig."

"I don't really know him all that well."

"That can be remedied in a heartbeat." Snapping her fingers, Daphne added, "Believe me, I know."

Chapter Five

"**I** was hoping you could help me work in the garage sometime soon," Sandra Bennett said.

The question, and the hesitant way she stated it, made Craig look up from the bowl of spaghetti he was eating. "Is there something you need, Mom?"

She twirled a noodle around her fork. "Nothing too earth shattering. It's just that Am Vets is stopping by at the end of the month. I think it's time I gave away some of your dad's old things."

Her words hit him like a hammer in the belly. "Really?"

"You know I still have all those tools of your dad's. It would be good to divest myself of most—I have no need for them."

54

He didn't like to think of yet another part of his dad disappearing. "They're still good to have on hand."

"Some are, but not all of them," she corrected. "I doubt I'll ever need a miter box or ten saws in an emergency. You know as well as I do that they're just taking up space. I want to install cabinets for my gardening supplies."

"I'll make room. I'll rearrange everything again."

"No. Craig, you know what a mess the garage is. Why, last winter I could hardly park my car inside."

It was hard to think of snow when the humidity seemed to keep him constantly damp. "I'll help you get better organized. Maybe all we need to do is—"

"It's time, Craig."

With a curious sense of dejection, he knew his mom was right. He hated to admit it, hated to even think it, but Craig knew that after two years, it was time for his mom to stop holding on to the past. "You sure?" he asked, asking for more than if she was ready to get rid of power tools. Asking if she was really ready to move on.

Craig had a feeling he was asking the same thing to himself.

"I'm sure. I don't know if there's anything in the garage that you need, Craig, but you're welcome to sort through it."

"Thanks. One night this week I'll come over and help you sort and clean."

"You'll have the time?" Wide blue eyes, so like his, peeked through her blonde bangs.

"Of course I will."

His mom set down her fork. "Craig, I was thinking that maybe it's time that you moved on too. I'm afraid that you've put your life on hold to take care of me. To take care of the rest of your family. And . . . we've let you."

He pushed his plate away, no longer hungry. "There hasn't been anything in my life that I had to put on hold. Besides, we're talking about you, not me."

"Craig. Now you're being silly."

"I promised Dad I'd look after you."

"You have. But, I'm better now."

He still felt defensive. "There's nothing wrong with helping out Leah or Lauren."

"You're a wonderful brother. And, there's nothing wrong with helping us out now and again. But I think you've been so busy worrying about us, you've been forgetting your own needs. It's time you got a life of your own, son."

Craig shifted, more than a little wary. "I know that. I will do more, when I want to. There just hasn't been a thing that couldn't be pushed aside for you."

"I appreciate that, you know I do. But maybe it's

time for you to push your family aside a little, when you've got plans."

"Mom—"

"When I was twenty-eight, I had two kids."

"I know that." Craig tried to look anywhere instead of his mother's concerned gaze. He so did not need this conversation. Again.

"You work all the time. When you're not, you're over helping the rest of us when you should be going out with a nice girl."

If he wasn't so appalled by the conversation, Craig would have cracked a comment about all the "bad" girls he'd been dating.

Though, come to think of it, he hadn't been seeing any of them, either.

With an easy pace that came from years of habit, his mom stood up, cleared their plates, then brought over two mugs of coffee. "Is there anyone you're interested in?"

"Not really."

"I think that's a shame."

"What happened to 'don't settle down like me, take some time to enjoy your youth'?"

She laughed as she went back to the kitchen, then returned with two thick slices of chocolate cake. "Maybe if I thought you were enjoying your youth I'd be saying that." Picking up her coffee, she blew delicately before taking a sip.

"I have been going out. I was dating Pam. Remember Pam?" he asked triumphantly, eager to prove to them both that he was perfectly capable of living his own life. "Pretty girl? Dark curly hair? Green eyes?"

"I do remember Pam," she said with a frown. "She adored you."

"You sound like that was a bad thing."

"It wasn't."

"Mom, if you're going to give me advice, at least be honest."

Carefully she slid her fork through the corner of the cake, her expression pleased as the corner clung to her fork. "I never thought of you two as sticking. But, there are a lot of other women in Payton. Maybe you should try a church group? You could meet a lot of nice women there."

"I don't think so."

"You need to go out someplace where there're women. I mean, it's not like you're going to meet anyone at your work site."

But, he had, hadn't he? Lindsay Flynn had caught his eye and stirred his body in a way that few women had lately. From the moment he saw her and looked into those big brown eyes, he'd been lost.

Too bad it had been a one-sided kind of thing.

Craig sipped his coffee, thinking that he hadn't been so uncomfortable during a really good meal for some time. What had he done to deserve this, anyway? All he'd been doing was making himself available. He'd spent the last two years doing odd jobs and helping out as much as he could. Shoot, he'd visited Brandon at the hospital more than the rest of his sisters had. Now, because of all this good behavior, his mom was acting like he should have been partying till all hours every night of the week.

It was yet another example of never being able to win. Standing up, he said, "I'll come over on Thursday night to help you with the garage."

"I'm sorry Craig, but Thursday's no good."

"Saturday morning?"

To his surprise, his mom got up and pulled out a new desk calendar from a pile on the kitchen counter. "Hold on, sweetie." Methodically, she opened it up and scanned the pages. Craig leaned over and tried to catch a glimpse. "Hmm." To his surprise, she'd written lots of notes and appointments on each day's square.

What *was* she doing every day?

"Hmm. I can't clean the garage on Saturday. Sunday's church, and I'm going to go to the annual picnic after the eleven o'clock service. What about Monday or Tuesday?"

Knowing that he could make up any hours on the job that he missed, he shrugged. "Either. Monday?"

"Monday will be fine. Could you make it early evening? I'm going to go to a dinner that evening for the historical society."

Her sudden social life gave him a start. "Sure."

"Super! I'll pencil you in."

Pencil? "Mom, when did all of this happen? When did you get so busy?" He pointed to the calendar, to the numerous penciled-in plans. "What are you doing all the time?"

"*Living,* Craig. I've decided to start living again. Part of what has comforted me since your father's passing has been my wonderful cache of memories with him. A few months ago I realized that I would have nothing to recall about the last year except for being grief stricken."

Blinking back a tear, she added, "And while I needed that year . . . it's time to do something more. Your father would have wanted that, Craig. Don't you think so?"

Craig nodded. His dad had been all about life. About living each day to the fullest. He was about taking risks and bending the rules.

It was time for both he and his mother to start living again.

Over the next couple of days, Craig thought a lot about his mom, her comments about living, and his own lack of a social life.

He thought about it as he and Jack finished framing the second floor, then plumbing the bathrooms. He thought about it when he played softball with a couple of the guys from work on Sunday morning. He thought about it as he biked on the trail through downtown Payton on Monday night after helping his mom with the garage.

Yeah, he was getting out . . . and it was getting pretty obvious that his efforts were lame.

Garage cleaning and catching fly balls didn't hold much appeal.

He needed to start dating again. Maybe his mom had a point when she'd reminded him that she'd been married for years by the time she was his age.

What did it matter if the only woman who he'd been attracted to lately was too busy for him? Surely there had to be a whole lot of other women who he could take out. He just had to find them. Though he'd never had much patience for singles' bars, he thought they might offer a chance to meet someone new.

He was walking home on Thursday afternoon when a petite lady in high-heeled sandals approached him. "Are you Craig Bennett, by any chance?"

Her forthright manner stopped him in his tracks. "I am."

"Oh, good! I'm Daphne Reece," she said, holding out her hand.

He took it. Scanning her face, he noticed faded blonde hair, pretty gray eyes. She had a pleased expression . . . really pleased, like she'd just won the lottery.

He didn't feel a bit of recognition. "I'm sorry, do I know you?"

"No, but we have a mutual friend." With a tentative smile, she said, "Do you have a minute to talk?"

Craig was filthy. His crew had spent the entire day shingling the roof in ninety degree heat. He'd sweated enough to wring out a washrag. His nose was sunburned, and for the last hour, all he'd been able to think about was drinking something cool. He wasn't fit company for a dog, let alone this perfectly dressed lady.

"Please—I won't keep you too long," she pleaded.

And, though his head knew better, he found he couldn't tell her no. "Sure."

She motioned to one of the many ornately designed benches that decorated Payton's streets. "Here's a spot." As soon as he sat down, she leaned forward. "So. Lindsay Flynn is a friend of ours."

Daphne Reece had tracked him down because of Lindsay? Craig knew he couldn't keep the surprised expression from his face. "Lindsay?"

"Yes. Lindsay is the sister of my youngest daughter's husband."

He filled in the name. "Ethan."

"That's right!" Daphne beamed. "I knew you'd understand our connection."

"Um. Actually, I don't really know Lindsay all that well."

"Sure you do. She said you two had lunch together."

His wariness increased. Had Lindsay made something up about him? Was she going to sue the construction company about her accident? "We did."

"Well, she had dinner with my husband Jim and I the other day . . . and she talked about you."

He had no idea why she would have. "Is there a problem?"

"No. Well, I guess you could maybe call it a problem. She told me how attractive she found you . . . and how she had no time for dating."

A new, cold sweat came to life on his body. Was Lindsay telling people that he'd asked her out and she'd shot him down? That sounded even more outlandish.

"Lindsay had a certain look in her eyes when she spoke of you," Daphne said with a gleam in her eye. "That look made me think that perhaps I should pay you a visit."

The whole conversation was creepy. "Look, I don't know what she told you, but nothing happened between us. That whole board thing was an accident. And lunch lasted twenty minutes, max."

As if suddenly realizing he was on the defensive, she held up a hand. "I'm sorry. Lindsay doesn't know I'm here. I just wanted to tell you that if you were interested in her . . . and I think you should be because she's darling . . . you're going to have to get creative."

"Excuse me?"

"Lindsay has the strangest idea that she should be working twenty-four-seven. She doesn't want to let her family down. I'm afraid if she doesn't take time off now and then she's going to go crazy." She leaned forward. "You know what they say about all work and no play."

"Um . . . yes."

"You, Craig, would be so good for her."

"You don't even know me."

"I want to, though. Tell me, are you dating anyone seriously?"

What was going on? How come everyone was so interested in his love life—or lack of one—all of sudden? "I just went through this with my mother the other night. I'm not going to do it with you too."

"I'm sorry, I didn't hear your answer. Are you? Dating?"

"No. Not at the moment."

"I think Lindsay would be perfect for you." She tapped her foot against the foot of the bench as she examined him from head to toe. "Have you ever had any interest in the performing arts?"

"I'm in construction. No."

"Oh, dear. Here, I was just thinking that if you were to take a part in Lindsay's new play, the two of you could spend some time together." Flashing him a hundred-watt smile, she said, "Wouldn't that be great?"

"I'm sorry, but this conversation is just too weird for me." He pointed to the bench, his grimy clothes. "I don't have conversations like this. Especially not when I really need a shower."

She looked crestfallen. "I'm sorry. I don't know what has gotten into me. Instinct, I guess. I have five children, and they're all married now. I've gotten too used to meddling." She peered at him. "Do you have a large family, Craig?"

"I do. I'm the oldest of five kids."

"Ah. So we have something in common." Standing up, she said, "Have you ever felt like you couldn't do enough for them? Even when they don't need you to?"

Too many images of his siblings floated through to disagree. "As a matter of fact, yes."

"I heard through the grapevine that you were in a car accident a few years ago."

"That's true. I was."

"It was serious, right?"

"The car was totaled. I broke my arm, but other than that I fared pretty well."

"I assume something like that would teach a person to never give up."

It had, not that he was going to share that tidbit with her. "This is different."

"Oh. Well, all right. I guess it is." She patted her thighs. "Let's just forget this conversation. Not that we met, because I did enjoy meeting you."

He stood up as well. "I did too," he replied, then couldn't believe that he meant it.

"Good-bye, Craig."

And with a little wave, Daphne turned around and left. Craig didn't know whether to laugh or just be really aggravated. Being in Lindsay's play just so he could date her? Yeah, right.

Craig Bennett in a play? Acting? As they said in Cincinnati, "When pigs fly . . ."

Chapter Six

"So, as you can read for yourself on the hand-outs, we'll begin auditions in one week. Pay careful attention to the practice schedules. If you can't make them, don't try out."

A shuffling of papers, followed by a low murmur of voices followed the last of Lindsay's instructions. Lindsay knew from past experience that she needed to give everyone assembled time to process the information, then to discuss options with friends before continuing.

Since her actors were busy people, with whole lives to organize, she had to be respectful of their needs.

As people stood up, got coffee, ran to the bath-rooms or outside to smoke, and the noise level grew,

Lindsay shook her head as she thought of the first play she put on.

She'd been so full of herself. So full of ideas and good intentions that she'd conveniently forgotten that she was the only person on salary. Everyone else was donating time and volunteering to help make the play a success. They hadn't appreciated her autocratic lectures, the deadlines that couldn't be moved, or the schedules that made no room for personal emergencies.

Luckily, Jane Berstrum, a very nice lady in her sixties, had pulled her aside one evening. In no-nonsense terms, she'd relayed to Lindsay that she was about to not only lose her cast, but all of her ticket holders if she didn't ease up a little bit.

At first, Lindsay had been irritated, but then, after she overheard a few people complaining about her, she held a meeting and apologized.

Taking Jane's advice, she asked for help with the schedules, and suddenly, the whole cast stopped fighting her and began to help make the project an overwhelming success.

When she'd directed *Scrooge,* her first play in Payton, they'd been under a fierce deadline, but Lindsay forced herself to allow plenty of time for her cast members to have a say in the production.

She was gratified to see that many of the performers from that production had shown up at that evening's meeting to hear about *The Ghost and Mrs. Muir.*

After fifteen minutes flew by, Lindsay stood up again and held out a hand. "May I have your attention, please?"

One by one, people stopped talking and took their seats.

Lindsay clicked on the microphone so everyone could hear her. "I know it's getting late and that many of you have early mornings tomorrow. So, let's finish up tonight in stages. If you need to leave, please feel free. On Friday, I'll post the audition schedules on the front door of the theater. They'll also be in the paper, and on our website."

About a dozen people stood up and carefully made their way out of the room. "If you have a general question, I'll try and answer a few right now. Finally, if you have a personal question, you can either call me or e-mail me at the numbers listed."

After glancing at everyone, she nodded to Lydia, her stage manager. "All righty, then. First question?"

Mrs. Mac, the well-known receptionist for Dr. Stratton Sawyer, raised her hand. "Tell us how you envision the play . . . lighthearted? Dark and magical? Romantic?"

"Well, to me, the play is all of those things. I'm hoping for lighthearted dialogue . . . two main characters to play up the romance aspects . . . and to play up the theater's history by making the sets in shades of lavenders and grays."

"What about the ghost? Is he still going to be a sea captain?"

"Definitely! I'm not going to mess with the original plot. It's perfection."

As more questions followed, others left, giving Lindsay a better view of some of the people who had attended the meeting. A couple of the wives and husbands were regular customers of Ethan's hardware store. Also in attendance was Missy Reece, one of Daphne Reece's daughters-in-law. Marianne McKinley—Daphne's best friend—and Marianne's husband, Baron, were there . . . and in the back corner, right behind a silk tree was . . . Craig Bennett?

As if on cue, he raised his head and met her gaze directly.

Lindsay felt as if she'd walked right on the set of a soundstage . . . everything felt so still and magical.

She was so shocked she could hardly think straight.

"Lindsay?" Missy Reece asked. "Did you hear my question?"

"Oh. Yes, I'm sorry. Missy, there will be a need for several small parts, which is an excellent way to be a part of things without giving a huge time commitment."

After a few more questions, Lindsay tapped the podium. "Thanks, everyone, for coming. I'll look forward to auditions next week."

From the corner of her eye, she watched Craig stand up, walk to the door, then with a determined look, turn back around and stride forward. It was all she could do to tear her gaze from him. Craig's jeans were riding low on his hips, faded and soft, and oh so masculine. His T-shirt managed to grip his muscles and set off his blue eyes like a costume designer had just outfitted him.

After she said good-bye to a few more people, he stepped close. The scent of soap and pine clung to him. His blond curls were damp from the shower. A faint outline of stubble clung to his cheeks. The purely masculine look made Lindsay's heart beat double-time. What was it about men who showered but didn't shave regularly that was so darn attractive?

"So, has anyone told you that you're pretty impressive on the stage?"

With great effort, she stopped staring at his cheeks and met his deep blue gaze. "Excuse me?"

He grinned. "I just wanted to give you a compliment. This was a pretty big crowd; there must have been close to sixty people in here. But everyone was looking to you for guidance. This is definitely where you need to be. I'm impressed."

Lindsay felt her cheeks heat at his praise. "Thanks. I was just thinking to myself that I was handling things better than I used to. I, uh, have a tendency to do things too quickly."

"If you produce a play like you walk, I'd say I can imagine that."

She took the comment for the gentle teasing it was, but couldn't resist teasing a little right back. "Hey!"

Craig held up his hands. "I don't mean any disrespect, but you've got to admit that you walk like you're in the middle of New York City—quickly and with a mission."

She laughed. "Ethan says it's annoying."

"I wouldn't say that." Tilting his head, he winked. "It's appealing, if you want to know the truth."

His praise, and the way he was looking at her, made Lindsay feel more than a little attracted to him.

Oh, who was she fooling? She'd been attracted to Craig from the moment she'd seen his face with his frame of blond curls. "What are you doing here?"

He shrugged. "I had some time off today and thought I'd stop by."

"Are you going to audition?"

"I don't know. I don't know if I'm the actor type. I was more interested in seeing how you were putting the whole thing together."

"I'm glad you stopped by." Her natural enthusiasm

getting the best of her, she added, "If you'd ever like to be a part of it, I think you should. You might be surprised how much fun it is to collectively put on a play. The camaraderie is infectious."

His gaze flicked to her mouth. "I can imagine how working together closely can be a good thing."

She swallowed hard. "Mm-hmm."

He gestured to the empty stage behind her. "Maybe I could help with the sets?"

"We could always use someone handy with tools. But since you work with your hands all day, perhaps you'd enjoy doing something completely different for a couple of weeks?"

"I might think about it, if I thought there might be someone in the cast who could give me some acting tips."

She couldn't resist flirting a little more. He was so attractive, and they were practically the only ones left in the building. "That could possibly be arranged," she murmured.

He ran one calloused finger along the top of her hand, as if he couldn't refrain another moment from touching her. "How about I skip the play and take you out instead? We could go for a walk along the bike path. Scare a few fireflies?"

Lindsay's heart slammed in her ribcage. Oh, it would be so easy to accept. It had been a long time since she'd been so attuned to another person, since she felt that fresh twist of longing, just like characters in old movies.

Craig was so handsome, and there was something about his blue eyes that made her want to say yes right away. How could she not want to walk with him at night? Alone except for the stars and fireflies?

She'd be a fool to pretend that it wouldn't be thrilling to kiss him, to be enfolded in his strong arms and feel the hard planes of his chest against her own.

She'd love to date him, to spend more time getting to know him. She knew he was athletic; maybe they could go on bike rides . . . or even down the Little Miami River in canoes?

But then reality stepped in again. They were so different . . . and she was too busy. And what if they did have a good time? She'd want to see him again. And again.

She was so compulsive. Other things, like the theater, would take second place, and that couldn't happen. She'd ruined a commitment before, and the harsh words from her first director in college still felt fresh and biting. There was no way she could put her career in jeopardy.

"Craig, it's not you. You stood right there when I told the crowd our schedule. It's going to get crazy, then blossom into lunacy." Steeling herself, she said,

"I just don't think I'm going to have a lot of extra time until after the play."

His hand had gone from stroking her skin to linking their fingers. "That's hardly fair to you or me."

"I know, but that's how it is. I'm afraid if I start something with you it's going to interfere with my work . . . or the other way around."

"I asked you out, not proposed."

Lindsay cringed inside as she knew he was exactly right. She was jumping to conclusions. But she felt something strong between them, strong enough to make her think of frequent dates and long kisses . . . and of easily blowing off responsibilities. "I'm sorry if I sound completely presumptuous. I just don't want to go down a path with different expectations." Trying to make him understand, she said, "I dated a guy last year, while I was working on *Scrooge*. I ended up forgetting a couple of activities he'd planned, and he was really hurt. I felt horrible. I don't want to do that to you."

Squeezing his hand, she said, "I'd hate it if I disappointed you." She hoped Craig could read everything she wasn't saying. Though they'd hardly had time to get to know each other, she knew she liked him. A lot.

"No matter what, I think you should consider being in the play, Craig. You might enjoy it, and it would be a great way for us to see each other."

"Maybe. Whatever." In a forced move, he dropped his hand, leaving hers suddenly free and cool. "Well. It's getting late. I better get going."

Disappointment rushed through her as she heard his good-bye. No way was he going to act in the play. Not that she could blame him, acting was tough, even in a local theater. It would be especially tough for someone who didn't take to performing naturally. And she had a strong suspicion Craig definitely did not. She didn't know of too many construction worker actors.

It was time to let him leave, for them to finally go their separate ways. "All right. Well, it was good seeing you. Really good."

Her words seemed to jar him. "I almost forgot to ask. Are you feeling better?"

She pointed to her arm, hoping he didn't notice the goose bumps that appeared under his gaze. "Hardly a scar," she murmured. "That little accident is now firmly in my past."

"I'm glad. Bye, Lindsay."

He walked away before she could say another word.

It was probably just as well, she reflected, cleaning up the chairs, and throwing away a couple of Styrofoam coffee cups.

If Craig was going to be there every day, she'd be forced to see him, which would probably mean that she wouldn't be able to think about anything else. It seemed that nothing in her body worked properly whenever he was around.

As she flicked off the theater's main switch for lights, Lindsay walked up the dim center aisle. And then was brought up short by the sudden burst of music from an unplugged boom box.

She stifled a squeal. Someone—or something—had paid a visit.

When Denise had lived there, she'd found comfort in imagining there was a ghostly presence. Lindsay felt completely the opposite. These mysterious phenomena scared her half to death!

"Are you ever going to like anything besides big band songs?" she asked the wisp of talcum powder, the only clue to the apparition. "How about a change of pace, like some country and western?"

No answer.

Because she was feeling peevish, she called out, "Rap? Blues? The Stones?"

Only an eerie stillness greeted her, Sally's version of the cold shoulder.

Feeling repentant, Lindsay turned off the lights. "Sorry. I guess you heard all that between Craig and me. It put me in a bad mood. I want to see Craig again so badly . . . but I'm too worried about failing to venture in full force. What if I mess everything up? How could I look at my brother? He's having to go to night school because my parents couldn't afford to send both of us at the same time. I attended classes while he worked construction. Now's he's given me this opportunity too. There's just no way I can even think about letting him down."

The lights flickered in silent commiseration.

As she trudged up the three flights of stairs to her cozy apartment, Lindsay sighed. "Maybe I should get a dog. Though it wouldn't answer me, either . . . at least I could look at it and pretend it was listening."

Chapter Seven

The burst of lightning flashing across the sky was what finally made Hal, their foreman, decide to cut the day short. "Hook 'em up, guys. I'm calling it."

With a muffled curse, Craig gathered his tools and an old Styrofoam coffee cup as he followed the rest of the crew to the back of the site. Cutting the day short because of rain wasn't a surprise, but it was never welcome news.

If they didn't work, they didn't get paid. Unless Hal let them do overtime later on in the week, each man was going to have a smaller paycheck than he was counting on.

Another bolt flashed, bringing with it the inevitable torrent of rain. In seconds, the temperature had dropped twenty degrees.

"Blasted rain," Craig said to no one in particular. His hair was plastered to his head, his boots felt like mini-lakes, and his cell phone had probably just lived its last day.

Grumblings surrounded him as he checked out with Hal. The day's lost wages were not something anyone was happy about.

Thunder clapped. Shaking his head, Craig joined Jack under the shelter of the back porch. Jack moved over to make room. "Might as well wait for a break," he said. "If we go out now, all we'll get is soaked to the skin."

"Like I'm not already."

Jack chuckled. "You bring your truck?"

"I did. I thought we'd be doing some trim work today, so I wanted my tool box."

"I brought mine too." Jack shook his head as they continued to watch the rain pour down in thick sheets. "This is all Maggie and I need. I need every penny to help pay for childcare this week. We had to use some of our savings when her car broke down last month."

"This is when you wish that someone would drive by and offer to hire us to work indoors for a day."

"I'd do about anything. Oh, well, I guess I can pick up the kids early, that will help out some." As another crash of thunder erupted, he turned to Craig. "What are you going to do?"

"Visit Brandon, I guess. My mom is out of town visiting my aunt."

Jack rolled his eyes. "You need a life, man. You're single, your car is paid for, you live in an apartment." Clapping him on the back, he added, "You've got it made! You should be watching SportsCenter or taking some girl out to the movies today." He waggled his eyebrows. "Or spending it doing far better things."

He groaned. It had been so long since Craig had done anything like that. He tried to take the high road. "Even us guys without lives have obligations. Brandon will be glad to see me."

"Yeah. I guess so." The wind shifted, bringing with it a break in the storm. "Here's my chance. See you tomorrow."

"See you." Craig would never admit it, but a part of him envied Jack's responsibilities. At least Jack knew that people were counting on him. And Maggie was great, a real partner. She worked as an aide in an elementary school and was a great mom. They were building a life together that they could look on with pride.

With a sigh, he stepped into the rain just as a fresh torrent blew again. As the rush of water plastered his hair, he figured it was a sign that once again, he was too late to do much of anything.

*   *   *

"Brandon's at school, silly," Leah chided him twenty minutes later. "I thought we told you that."

Craig couldn't believe he was actually feeling bad that Brandon had recovered. "I guess I forgot."

Gripping his hand, she tugged it. "You look like a wet rat. Come on in and I'll feed you lunch. Want some soup?"

Peevishly, Craig refused. "Nah, I'll just get going."

"You sure? It's no trouble to open up another can."

"Positive."

"What are you going to do for the rest of the day?"

That was the question of the day. "I don't know."

"Only you would have a day free and make it into a problem."

"I'm not making it a problem . . . I just was trying to check on Brandon, that's all."

"You're right. I'm sorry. You're always here for us, and for Mom. I probably don't thank you enough."

"You don't need to." Craig couldn't stand there another minute. A sixth sense told him that Leah was about to jump on the 'Craig needs a life' bandwagon, and he didn't think he was up for hearing it from one more person. "I'll see you soon, Leah. Let me know if you need anything."

"I will. You do the same."

"Me? I don't need a thing."

"But, maybe there's something you *want* that I could help with?"

Craig chuckled as he strode back to his truck. That had been a favorite saying of his dad's . . . that you can't live life just by needs. Sometimes what you want was just as important.

As he drove back through the streets of Payton to his apartment, he passed the theater. Lit up like the proverbial Christmas tree, it shone like a beacon in the dreary weather. Seeing no one behind him, he slowed down to see what was going on.

A banner with writing in bold purple block letters hung across the front entrance: TRYOUTS TODAY FOR GHOST AND MRS. MUIR

Maybe it was because he had no desire to go sit by himself with his own can of soup. Maybe it was because everyone from his best friend to his mother was saying he needed to do more than just work and help his family.

Maybe it was because no matter how much Lindsay had protested, he knew there was something special between them that needed exploring.

If she didn't think they had time, he'd show her that they had nothing but time. A whole future ahead of them.

For whatever reason, he pulled over and quickly parallel parked. Feeling like a firefighter entering a burning building, Craig inhaled deeply, and pushed aside his doubts.

He was going in.

Chapter Eight

Now, why couldn't anything in her life go smoothly? It was raining cats and dogs outside, making the humidity in the old theater go through the roof. The rain was also making everyone late.

Lindsay was doing her best to be understanding, but the situation was almost out of control. They had a ton of read-throughs to get to, and a limited time to get to them.

Impatiently, Lindsay checked her clipboard again as forty people milled the aisles of the theater, in no hurry to get situated. She glanced toward Denise and Ethan for help.

Well, Denise at least. Ethan had made it clear from the moment he appeared on the premises that he was only there for emotional support and pizza ordering.

Denise, dressed in white shorts and a cute teal colored sweater set, stood in the back corner. She held a clipboard, too, but it hung at her side as she chatted with a group of women. When they all burst into laughter, Lindsay couldn't help but scowl.

Denise's ease with unexpected situations was in direct contrast to Lindsay's nervous state. And it grated on her just like a roll of sandpaper.

"Denise?" Lindsay called out. "Could I bother you for a moment?"

"Oh. Sure. Good luck," she said to the women before stepping forward. "What's up? You look stressed out."

"I have every reason to be. Everything's a mess."

Denise scanned the room before turning back to her. "No it's not. Tryouts are about to start, a team of judges is in the back room getting fortified with coffee, and we've got a great turnout. Everything's terrific!"

"The rain is a bad omen. The play's going to be a failure."

"Oh, you theater types. So superstitious. The rain is a sign that my begonias aren't going to dry up and die today. Chin up. We're getting there."

"I feel like it's all gotten the best of me."

"Don't." Denise pulled over a portable microphone unit. "Here. Put it to good use. I'll do my best to handle crowd control."

Warily, Lindsay tapped the head of the microphone. It squawked, effectively silencing the whole room in an instant. "We'll go ahead and begin auditions now. Please make sure you have your photo, along with your personal information contact sheet with you when you go into the tryout rooms," she instructed. "Depending on the judges' recommendations, we should have our selection for the entire cast posted in three days."

Her confidence back in hand, Lindsay scanned the room. "Please go down the back hallway and into my office if you're interested in reading for the part of Mrs. Muir. All Captain and Martha parts need to report to the green room. Everyone else, stay here. You'll read on the stage."

Groans erupted. Most preferred auditioning in private, but there was no other way to manage things, especially with the rain. Chuckling, she said, "It won't be so bad. We're a great audience for each other. Good luck, everyone."

As soon as she turned off the microphone, her brother approached. "Great job."

"Thanks."

"What can I do?"

She glanced at her notes. "I need you to check on the judges to make sure they're moving things along at a good clip, and to direct any latecomers."

"Speaking of that, here's one more," Ethan said as the heavy front door opened once again.

Lindsay blinked as she was sure her eyes deceived her. Craig Bennett?

Ethan acted like the guy was his long lost brother. "Craig! Buddy, how are you?"

Craig looked like he'd swallowed a goldfish. "All right."

Ethan pointed to his damp T-shirt and shorts. "You're soaked."

"I was at the site when the downpour came."

"Too bad. What are you doing here?"

Glancing at Lindsay, Craig shrugged. "Trying out."

Ethan's eyebrows rose almost to his hairline. "No kidding?"

"I'm glad you're here," she said sincerely. Though she'd said she didn't want to date, she hadn't been able to stop thinking of Craig. Just the idea of being around him more often made her mood improve. Truly pleased, Lindsay stepped in before her brother did something to scare him away. "What part do you want to audition for?"

"Something small."

She scanned the cast list. "How about Mr. Sproule's

agent or Bill, Anna's fiance? Both of them are in a couple of scenes, but only say about ten lines total."

He shifted. Met her gaze and held on tight. "Sure," he murmured. "Whatever you want me to do . . . I'll do."

Ethan was still looking at Craig like he'd just grown two more feet. "I didn't know you were into acting."

"I didn't think I was, either," Craig said, never taking his eyes off of Lindsay. "But lately, it's come to my attention that I should probably get out more."

"I'm surprised you didn't just want to take up running."

Craig glared. "It's raining."

Before Ethan could think of another activity for Craig to do, Lindsay flipped through a stack of scripts sitting on an old table nearby. Pulling one out, she handed it to him. "Here. Go read through this, then give your name to Denise. She's the petite gal in front with the clipboard."

Craig scanned the instructions on the front cover. "Maybe I should leave. I don't have any experience . . . or even a picture."

"No! I mean, I know what you look like, Craig. Don't worry about a photo."

Ethan whistled low.

Craig exchanged a glance with Ethan. Ethan grinned. "So—that's how it is. Good luck."

"Thanks." Craig walked toward one of the tryout rooms.

As Lindsay watched him leave, she felt she was being watched again, but this time it was the brotherly kind, not otherworldly.

"So . . . how well do you know Craig?" he asked, his voice filled with amusement.

"Not too well. I got injured at his construction site. He helped me."

"It looks like there's more between the two of you than that. Are you two dating?"

"No."

He narrowed his eyes. "You sure said that quickly."

Though she had no desire to explain herself to her brother, she knew Ethan wouldn't give her a minute's peace if she didn't try. "We've gone to get a burger together. He's asked me out."

"Good. What are you two going to do?"

Somehow, knowing that Ethan liked Craig made her even more uncomfortable. "Actually, nothing. I said no."

"Why?"

"Well, I'm pretty busy."

Ethan kept talking. "Craig's a great guy. I don't know him real well, but he's got a good reputation."

"You just like him because he's a guy's guy and likes NASCAR and power tools."

"Nothing wrong with any of those things."

"You're right, there's not. I said no because I knew I was going to be busy with the play."

"Busy with the play?" Ethan brushed a hand through his hair. "You can still go out to eat, right?"

"You know how I get . . . I start living and breathing the thing."

"And we both know that's not healthy, right?"

She slumped. "Right. But I want it to go well. I don't want to let Denise down." *Or you, Ethan,* she wanted to add, but didn't. He would just get embarrassed about the whole college thing, and she would get embarrassed for bringing it up.

"You would never let Denise down; she thinks you're great. She knows you're working hard."

"She won't if I mess this play up."

"Linds—"

"Lindsay, we're ready!" Denise called out.

"That's my cue," Lindsay said in a rush. "I've got to go."

"Saved by the bell," Ethan muttered as Lindsay pretended she didn't hear him. And pretended she wasn't thrilled to see Craig once again.

Craig gripped his paper as he waited for his chance to go up onstage. The other people around him made the whole process look so easy. They chatted, ran lines. Most people in the room had been in other plays before. Several had had parts in *Scrooge*. He tried not to care that he'd never even spoken in front of other people since his pitiful run for student council vice president his junior year in high school. But still, a nagging feeling of worry stewed as the people around him shared theatrical stories while waiting for their turn.

Closing his eyes, Craig hoped for patience. He didn't care how well he performed. The play didn't mean a thing to him, not really. He just wanted an excuse to be near Lindsay.

"Craig Bennett?"

Automatically, he turned to see who called him. It was Denise Flynn from up on the stage.

He'd climbed rock faces for fun. He'd scuba dived along coral reefs. He'd worked in four- and five-story buildings with little or no support.

None of those experiences even came close to what he was feeling at the moment: sheer panic.

"Craig Bennett?" Denise repeated. "Craig?"

He raised his arm like he was still back in high school. "Here."

Denise Flynn laughed. "Are you ready for your reading?"

"Oh. Sure." With measured steps, he approached the stage, turning to his left like a soldier when Denise discreetly motioned to him where the stairs were.

An *X* made of colored masking tape marked where he was supposed to go. Clutching his script, he strode to the spot.

"Craig, as I'm sure you're aware, I'll be reading the part of Lucy. You're the assistant at the publisher's."

"All right." Craig took a deep breath and tried hard to remember that he didn't care about the play. At all.

Denise caught his eye. "So, whenever you're ready?"

Even though common sense told him differently, Craig felt as if every person in the whole building had stopped what they were doing and had turned to stare at him. This was worse than any class he'd had in high school. His tongue felt thick and his mouth felt dry.

Like a ventriloquist's dummy, he stared at Denise.

She smiled, her expression warm and reassuring. "This isn't Broadway—just a roomful of volunteers. No one's expecting Lionel Barrymore. Relax."

Forcing a chuckle, Craig rolled his shoulders. Denise was right. There was nobody in here whom he had to impress . . . unless it was someone with ash-colored hair and long legs. "Sorry. This is my first time."

"Everyone has one," she quipped. Pointing to the *X,* she said, "Take your mark."

He did as he was told. Mercifully, Denise stepped

forward, standing almost directly across from him. She read Lucy's lines in such a way that it seemed like they were having a conversation. Craig finally spoke. "Do you have an appointment?"

Denise eyed her script. "No," she read. "Will that be a problem?"

All of the sudden, it felt as if his role cloaked him. He no longer cared so much about the audience, what they thought . . . or even if Lindsay was nearby. He relaxed and said his lines in a more natural way, like they actually meant something to him.

As they volleyed their lines, Craig even attempted to put a little emotion into his words.

Denise smiled encouragement as she spoke again. After a few more minutes, they were done. His audition was over.

"You did great, Craig," she said.

He laughed. "We both know I didn't . . . but it was a good experience. Easier than I thought it would be."

"You survived."

As another woman called the next person to the stage, Denise walked toward him back to the stairs. "If you don't mind my asking, what made you decide to do this?"

"Couple of things."

Her lips tilted up. "Care to share?"

"Lately, more than one person has told me that I

should try new things." He had no desire to admit that he was really only doing this because it was raining—and he wanted to spend time with Lindsay.

To Craig's surprise, Denise seemed to take his reason at face value. "Community theater is a great way to become more involved. It's sure helped me overcome my shyness." Examining her clipboard, she said, "Now, Lindsay said you didn't arrive with any paperwork. May I get your contact information from you?"

"Sure." Craig gave her his cell and e-mail address, then said good-bye as she turned to greet the next hopeful cast member. He was just looking around, admiring the ornate lines of the vintage theater, when Lindsay appeared.

"I was hoping I'd catch you before you left," she said.

A thrill of pleasure—and embarrassment—pooled into his gut. "You watched me audition?"

"Yep. I was standing offstage. You were great, Craig."

"I wasn't great. But, thanks. We'll see if I was good enough."

She winked. "You might be surprised to find that someone here with pull is rooting for you."

Her words and her flirty manner surprised him. "This is a change from our last meeting."

"Is it?"

"It is." Stepping close enough to catch her scent, he murmured, "I thought you didn't care about me . . . or seeing me again."

"That's not true. I do care. I just can't date right now." She glanced at his lips, at his bicep, then looked down and fiddled with her clipboard. "For the next two months, I'll be here almost every night, working on the play."

"And then?"

Her eyes widened. "Well, then there's all the other things to do. Tickets to print and flyers to design."

When she fussed with her clipboard again, Craig gave in to temptation and covered her fingers with his own. Immediately, her hand stilled, warming under his. "You're going to be busy."

"I am."

The sharp bark of laughter down the hall reminded them both that they were far from alone. Lindsay stepped back, effectively breaking their contact. "But, if you're here, we'll see each other sometimes."

"Sometimes?"

"Probably more than that. I won't be able to avoid you."

"I hope not." Craig knew there was no way she would be able to avoid him if he was in the play. He'd stick to her like glue.

She swallowed. "Actually, I'd love to see you here.

I can't believe you auditioned. I couldn't believe it when I saw you walk through that front door. It was like a gift."

A gift? Her metaphor gave him a start, but he, also felt that the same way. There was something unique between them. Something worth investigating. Even worth embarrassing himself for. "If I do get a part, I'll be glad to help you in any way I can." Because he wanted to touch her again, he brushed a stray lock of hair away from her neck. Lowering his voice, he said, "I don't know if anyone's told you . . . but I'm great at menial tasks."

Her breath hitched before she swallowed hard. "I'll remember that." She gestured to the entryway. "This sure is a pretty building, isn't it?"

He didn't take his eyes off of her. "Very."

She cleared her throat. "Would you like a tour?"

"Do you have time?"

"Not tonight . . . but tomorrow evening I will. Any chance you might be free?"

"I could probably fit a tour in."

"Come by at seven?"

"I'll be here."

As if in slow-motion, Craig watched Lindsay finally stop fiddling with her clipboard and lay a hand on his arm, her long fingers cool and feminine against his skin. "I'll be here too," she said.

"Linds?" Denise called out. "You around?"

As if on fire, Lindsay's hand dropped. "That's my cue."

Craig just nodded as she trotted back to the stage. Auditioning for the play had been totally worth it. He liked Lindsay Flynn. He liked her a lot.

As he stepped back into the pouring rain, he almost welcomed the cold sting against his skin.

Chapter Nine

For three hours, they'd been dissecting the auditions and casting parts. On a large white board, cast members were listed, along with photos of each person. This time, the main parts had been chosen with ease; it was the secondary roles that were giving Lindsay, Denise, Ethan, and Daphne Reece fits.

Lindsay's hand faltered as Daphne Reece turned to her. "So, in what part should we cast Craig Bennett?" the older lady asked. Dressed to the nines as usual, Daphne had been nothing but professional and pleasant the entire evening.

Lindsay was grateful for her assistance, which made it kind of strange how proprietary she felt about Craig.

She felt so happy . . . it wasn't everyday that a man she liked was willing to do so much just to be with her. She felt like jumping for joy, walking on the moon.

Hoping to keep her voice steady, she said as calmly as she dared, "I think he would do well as the publisher's assistant. That's the one he read for."

"Really? He's so cute. Maybe he should be the publisher. He has more lines."

The scatterbrained comment stayed with her. Cute? Craig Bennett was far more than that. He was gorgeous. Extremely attractive.

Not that anybody but her ought to be thinking that.

A tiny stab of jealousy billowed up and tried to catch hold of her reasoning abilities. Lindsay did her best to tamp it firmly back. "I don't think Craig is ready for a big role. The assistant's part is good. The character doesn't show a lot of emotion and mainly just stands around. But, he's important because he connects with the audience."

Denise leaned forward. "Are we talking about Craig or the character being important?"

Lindsay didn't care for Denise's sly expression. "Both, of course."

Denise looked at her husband. "Of course."

"Of course," Ethan echoed with a smirk.

The last thing Lindsay needed was Ethan acting like an annoying older brother. "We're just friends."

"I have a feeling there's more to the two of you than that."

Ethan's words made Lindsay want to agree, though she was afraid to take anything for granted. As much as she wanted to hope that they could have a future together, she was also too much of a realist to count on it. Besides, she had a five-year plan that had nothing in it about falling in love. If she did go into a relationship, Lindsay wouldn't be able to give it her all, and she'd end up hurting his feelings.

Daphne flipped through the papers again, then examined the large poster board on Lindsay's office wall. There, every part was listed. Photos of actors already chosen were pinned next to the names. Creating a cast this way enabled all of them to visualize what the ensemble might look like when they were together.

It also gave Lindsay another way to make sure she had a wide assortment of cast members. She liked to have both old and new members, as well as a good mixture of experienced and inexperienced actors. There were also personality issues to consider in their type of situation too. Putting on a play was no exact science. Things got lost, mistakes were made, and real life also came into play.

One time she'd completely forgotten the major road construction and scheduled a series of rehearsals in the midst of the most traffic congested time of the day. When people hadn't shown up on time, it had thrown a lot of other schedules off, and Lindsay had ended up taking her frustrations out on the people who had been there.

Needless to say, it had been yet another learning experience.

"What do you think about the cast now?" Denise asked, as she pinned up the photo of Mrs. Mac who they'd unanimously agreed would be the best Angelica, the mother-in-law.

"I think it looks fine," Lindsay said. "We've got some really good people in key parts, and others who've been wanting to play bigger roles in the production too."

After taking some notes, Denise said, "Let's move on. We need to set up the committees for costumes, scene construction, and publicity and sales."

"That's already taken care of," Missy Reece said from her position in the back of the room. "Since I was only needed as an observer today, I talked to people and organized the committees in my spare time."

"You are so amazing, Missy," Lindsay said. "I thought I was organized. But you take things to new limits."

"It's both a blessing and a curse," Missy admitted. "Kevin's told me that I can get too involved in minute details."

Daphne, Missy's mother-in-law sat up straighter.

"My son told you that? Obviously we need to share some words."

"Don't say anything," Missy pleaded with a grin. "No need to get involved."

Lindsay watched Denise start laughing. "Look out, Miss. Mom needs somebody's life to meddle with. Joanne hasn't had her baby yet, and Ethan and I are doing too well for her tastes."

"Stop, you girls. I never meddle where I'm not wanted. Do I, Lindsay?" Mrs. Reece winked.

"What's that supposed to mean?" Denise asked. As a spark of understanding dawned, she narrowed her eyes. "Oh my goodness. Is Mom already involved in your love life?"

Daphne tapped her pencil on the table. "*Involvement* is a strong word."

"Is that really why Craig was here?" Denise asked.

"I'm not dating anybody."

Missy sighed. "Someone needs to fill me in. I'm confused."

"Don't be. Nothing's going on."

"I wouldn't say that," Daphne interjected. "After all, Craig did show up for auditions."

Lindsay stared at Denise for a split second before turning to Mrs. Reece. "You had something to do with that?"

"Only a little bit. I told him that it would be in his

best interests if he got involved, so he could spend some time with you."

"Oh, Daphne."

"Oh, Lindsay," Missy said, shaking her head. "Get ready."

"How did all of this happen, Mom?" Denise asked.

"Nothing too earth-shattering. I just waited until he was leaving work the other day and flagged him down on the street." She waved a hand across her chest. "My goodness, that man is handsome. He must exercise constantly. Did any of you know that he walks to work most days?"

"You're incorrigible, Mom," Denise said.

"But not off track. You were happy to see him here, weren't you, Lindsay?"

She had been until she'd found out that he hadn't shown up of his own accord. "I'm completely embarrassed. I acted like I was doing him such a big favor." With a moan, she added, "Oh my gosh. I told him that being in the play would be a great opportunity for him!"

"I talked to him, too, Lindsay," Ethan said. "Believe me, he wasn't here out of coercion."

"Coercion!" Daphne Reece pursed her lips. "I didn't coerce any one."

"I'm sorry, Lindsay," Missy said sincerely. "I know Daphne really was trying to help."

"Don't apologize, Missy," Denise said. "You didn't do a thing wrong. Mom meddles all the time. We all know that."

Daphne's face fell as the lot of them battered back and forth. "Children, stop it."

"Children?" Ethan grinned. "I'm thirty years old."

"You know what I mean. I take exception to your words. I'm a very good mom."

"You are," Denise replied. "I admit that freely."

"And a very good mother-in-law," Missy added. "It's just that it's hard to fall in love with someone coaching you from the sidelines. Kevin would agree."

Tired of the family squabble, Lindsay waved her hands. "Excuse me. This is *my* love life we're talking about." Or lack there of. For a little bit, she'd thought she was going to have a chance at love.

"I saw the two of you together," Missy said. "No way was he here because someone told him to."

Ethan chimed in. "Honestly, Lindsay. Does Craig Bennett look like the kind of guy to take the advice of a stranger?"

"No."

"All I did was mention that you were going to be at the theater a lot, and if he wanted to see you, he should get there, too," Daphne said once again. "I didn't do anything at all."

"Nothing besides meddle," Denise said.

Daphne eased her reading glasses onto her nose. "Need I remind you that we have a schedule to iron out?"

"Where are you off to, Craig?" Jack called out as Craig gathered up his tools at 5:01 on the dot.

His hands slowed. He was going to play practice, but no way was he going to share that out loud. The guys on the crew were like most other construction workers he'd ever met. They loved practical jokes. Finding out that he was dressing up and parading around on a stage would be ammunition for years to come. "Nowhere special."

"Why don't you come out with us? We're going to run to the Grill for burgers and beer."

"I don't think so."

"You sure? They've got two-for-one beers tonight."

Though a beer sounded pretty good after the hot, long day's work he'd put in, there was no way he could spare the time. "Sorry."

Jack shrugged. "Suit yourself, but remind me to tell you later about Maggie's friend. She wants to meet you soon."

Craig tried to be interested. "Really?"

"Yep. Her name's Christy and she's a postal worker." Jack grinned. "She's got a figure like you wouldn't believe."

There was only one lady he was thinking about,

and she looked perfect to him. Hoisting his tool belt over one shoulder, he walked toward the door. "Sorry, but I've got to go."

"All right."

Craig clocked out, then headed down the street. The first rehearsal started at six P.M. and when Lindsay had called him to let him know he'd gotten a part, she'd warned him that practices usually went long.

Today was the first read-through. It was an opportunity for the cast members to see each other and get a feel for how the whole play would feel. Whatever that meant.

Lindsay warned him to eat dinner beforehand. Craig was starving, but a cold shower and fresh clothes were on the agenda first.

Craig winced as he turned on the ignition of his F150, then hastily rolled down the windows. The August heat wasn't any better than July's and word on the news was that September wasn't supposed to be much better.

Within minutes, he pulled onto his street, parked, then finally made his way to his top-floor apartment above a furniture store. Craig wondered if his other job was going to be more lucrative than last winter. For the last two years, he removed snow with his uncle in the mornings, then tried to keep his days full with basement remodeling.

"Hey, Craig," his neighbor Andy called out as he

unlocked the door. Andy was recently retired and kept a close eye on the weather and the weather predictions. "Hot as can be outside today."

"Too hot for me."

"Tomorrow it'll be cooler."

"I'll look forward to it."

The cool air of his air-conditioner blasted him a greeting. Craig was tempted to sit and relax, but he was afraid he wouldn't get back up.

He quickly showered, threw on clean shorts and a T-shirt, and started making two sandwiches as he pushed the buttons on his answering machine.

He had three new messages. "Craig, it's Leah. Could you give me a call?"

The next was also from Leah. One from Lanie followed. Each sounded urgent. His stomach knotted as he pressed speed dial.

Leah answered her cell phone on the first ring. "Oh Craig, I'm so glad you called back. Brandon's back in the hospital."

Feeling like he'd been kicked in the ribs, he moved to the kitchen table, all thoughts of sandwiches and play practice forgotten. "What happened?"

"He caught a second bout of pneumonia. The doctor said his immunity system was weak, and being back in school didn't help things."

Leah sounded so tired and disappointed. "What do you need?" Craig asked.

"Could you go stop by soon? Maybe even tonight? I'm trying to keep his spirits up, but you know how it is with a ten-year-old. Moms are great with nursing, but not as much when it comes to joking around."

"Sure," he said automatically. "I'll be over within the hour." Leaning his head back, he shook it in frustration. Of course he was needed just when he'd decided to concentrate on himself.

Leah cleared her throat. "Craig? Are you okay? You sound funny. Oh, did you already have plans?"

He couldn't lie completely. "None that couldn't be broken. Believe it or not, I've got play practice. I, uh, tried out for a play. *The Ghost and Mrs. Muir,*" he added.

"What?"

Craig fought a smile. Her little screech was the first burst of humor he'd heard in her tone since their conversation began.

Because he liked making her smile, he briefly explained the conversations he'd had with his mom and Lindsay.

"That's when I decided that I needed to do something, Leah. Plus, I like Lindsay," he admitted. "She's different than any other woman I've ever met, but there's something about her that makes me want to try everything I can to make our relationship work."

"It's probably because she's not following you around, all moony," Leah said.

"Moony?"

"Sorry. 'Moony' is from Brandon's vocabulary. It means starry-eyed and silly." She chuckled. "Whatever. In any case, you know what I mean. With looks like yours, you've always had women make things easy for you."

He hated to complain, but having women constantly making blatant plays was not fun. "Not that easy."

"Easy enough. Craig, I love you, but you're far too good-looking for the average woman to ignore. Add that you're a construction worker, and girls start thinking about you like they're in that Diet Coke commercial. I think you needed a challenge."

"I can honestly say that Lindsay's never looked at me like I'm a catch."

"She must be the one," Leah said with glee. "I can't wait to meet her. Listen, why don't you just come by tomorrow? You've got to go to your play practice."

"No, I don't. I'll give Lindsay a call and let her know I can't make it."

"But—"

"Leah, there's no way I'm not going to see you and Brandon."

"We'll still be here tomorrow."

He closed his eyes. He hated to hear that. "I'm not going to disappoint you or my favorite nephew."

"Craig—"

"Leah, I'm glad you called. I am. Really. I'll be by the hospital within the hour."

"I'm sorry."

"I'm your brother. Don't be."

After he hung up, Craig quickly ate his sandwiches, then pulled out the flyer describing the rehearsals. When he found Lindsay Flynn's name, he wondered if maybe she'd been right all along. Sometimes life was just too complicated and busy to find time for love or romance.

With more than a little reluctance, he picked up the phone and dialed her number.

Chapter Ten

Lindsay groaned when the phone rang. All day, as soon as she started a project, it would shrill importantly, knocking off her concentration. When it rang yet again, Lindsay glanced at the caller ID, hoping she could ignore whoever was on the other end.

Craig Bennett was on the line! She quickly picked up the receiver. "Hello?"

"Lindsay, Craig Bennett."

"Hi," she said, telling herself to keep her voice as calm as possible. She glanced at her watch. "Did you have any questions? We're supposed to meet in an hour."

"Just one. How mad are you going to be if I can't make it?"

"I don't know." Because she couldn't tell if he was

111

teasing or not, she said, "Maybe a little bit. I try to keep close to the schedule I handed out because so many people have a lot of other commitments." When he didn't say anything, she added, "Tonight's meeting is pretty important. It's the first time everyone gets to see each other as a cast."

"Well, I guess I'm going to have to get ready for the wrath of Lindsay. I'm going to be at least an hour late getting there." He paused. "Maybe two."

"Why even show up?" The wisecrack was out before she could take it back. Frowning, Lindsay struggled to rephrase her comments. "I mean—"

"Maybe I shouldn't be in the play?" His voice had cooled considerably.

"I'm sorry for that joke," she apologized. "If you want to be here, of course I want you to come. What's going on? I mean, if you can share."

"My nephew Brandon is in the hospital again. Leah, my sister is a little strung out about it. Her husband's out of town. I need to stop by and see both of them."

Lindsay slapped her hand on her stack of papers, wishing she'd noticed something in his tone and been more sympathetic from the first. "Of course you do."

"You're okay with that?"

His surprise hurt her feelings. "Craig, just because

I live for this play doesn't mean I expect everyone else to. I'm not *that* inconsiderate. At least, I hope I'm not."

She heard his sigh on the other end. "I'm sorry if I sound stressed out. I left work right on time to be at practice, but when I got home, Leah had a string of messages waiting for me on my answering machine. To tell you the truth, I'm worried about her. She sounds exhausted. I didn't mean to bite your head off."

Still trying to make things work between them, she suggested, "Would you like to stop by later? Even if we're done, I'll be here." Thinking quickly, she added, "I could fill you in."

"Okay, sure. I'll do that."

Relieved that he sounded more like his familiar self, she said, "If you get here earlier than planned, you can find us in the auditorium. I'll see you later."

"Great. Bye."

When he hung up, Lindsay swallowed back a whole host of regrets. Though they'd finished the conversation on a good note, in the beginning, she'd said all the wrong things.

Gosh, had she even asked why his nephew was in the hospital?

As she recalled their conversation, it was terribly evident that she had not. No, at first, all she'd done was react to his curtness, and think about how his absence was going to affect her.

Not something to be very proud of. Her mother, who always had time for everyone, would be shaking her head in regret.

So would Ethan, who'd always put her needs before his own.

Unable to sit still a moment longer, Lindsay glanced at the clock. A quarter after five. Though it was early, Lindsay decided to go downstairs and get ready for the first big meeting. Coffee needed to be made in the green room, chairs and tables readied and organized for the thirty or so people who would be arriving within the hour.

Usually, she loved this first reading. She loved the excitement and optimism that prevailed in the atmosphere. New friendships were forged, old ones renewed. Everyone was fresh and rested and not stressed . . . at least not by the play.

As the weeks wore on, those things would change. People would start to get testy, nerves and emotions would take over.

As she walked down the stairs, Lindsay frowned. That's what she should have told Craig about. How she was so excited about this important night.

Maybe she could even have taken a chance and admitted that she was really excited to spend some time with him over the next few weeks. She'd been looking forward to having her own romance while staging *The Ghost and Mrs. Muir.*

An eerie feeling fell over her as she entered the green room. For a split second, she wondered if the ghost was paying another visit. The feeling, on top of her disappointing conversation with Craig, made her feel even more uptight.

She hoped things would turn around soon.

"When Jerry said he was going to have to be gone for the week, I didn't have the heart to tell him that I couldn't handle it," Leah admitted to Craig as they wandered to the elevator to get a cup of coffee.

"Brandon wasn't in the hospital when he booked the plane tickets. I'm sure he'd understand if you asked him to head on home early."

Leah shook her head. "I just don't think I can do that. Plus, he's already taken time off—we need the money. It's not like Brandon and I haven't been through this before. I'll be fine."

Craig clasped his sister's hand. "You don't have to be so strong, you know. Mom's here too."

Leah nodded as the elevator chimed and they stepped in. After pushing *G,* she turned to Craig as the doors slid closed. "And everybody else is on the way. Lanie called Curt. Lauren and Uncle Mike will visit tomorrow."

As the elevator doors slid open again, Craig

wrapped an arm over her shoulders as they entered the food court. "Let's get some coffee and sit down. Mom's got Brandon occupied with the video she brought and she told you to go get some dinner and relax before sitting with Brandon again."

"Thank goodness she was free tonight. Mom's so great."

"She is."

After grabbing their coffee cups, Craig paid, then followed Leah to a spot near the window. Below, the hilly landscape of downtown Cincinnati greeted them with a breathtaking sunset.

After commenting on the sunset and taking a few fortifying sips of coffee, Leah said, "I wouldn't say she's thrived after Dad's death . . . but she has become stronger. Don't you think?"

"Definitely. She told me that it was time for her to move on."

"She told me that, too, when I asked her to stay with us for the long weekend." Leah sipped again. "If you want to know the truth, part of me wasn't very happy to hear that she was doing so well or making a bunch of new friends. I guess I wanted her to keep missing Dad."

"I wasn't too happy either at first," Craig admitted. "But, she's right. We all need to continue our lives. Dad would have wanted that."

"I think she's joined a group for singles."

"Really?" Craig wasn't sure how he felt about that.

"She's not saying much, but I get the feeling that she's met some nice people." Leah frowned. "I'm kind of wondering whether I'm happy or sad about that too. Isn't that awful? I thought I'd be more supportive."

Craig knew the feeling. "I never pictured her dating again. 'Course, I always thought things would stay the same," he said as they picked up their cups and headed back to Brandon's room.

"Me too."

He divulged a little more. "I've tried to be there for her. But I'm starting to realize she needs us for emotional support too. I've been taking out her trash, helping with home repairs . . . but I haven't been as eager to listen to her tell me how lonely she is."

"I've been just as guilty." Crossing her arms across her chest, Leah said, "I was just telling Brandon on Sunday night that things were going to get back to normal, that I felt sure he was almost completely better. Now, here we are, just like a few weeks ago. I guess life has a way of changing your plans, huh?"

"It does." The talk of plans made Craig frown. Lindsay was probably wondering if he was ever going to show up. "I probably need to go soon."

Her eyes brightened. "Oh yeah! You've got your play rehearsal."

By mutual agreement, they walked toward Brandon's room. "I still can't believe I'm going to act in a play."

"No. But I'm happy you are. It sounds like fun."

"It sounds like a big mistake, more likely." Briefly, he filled Leah in on his latest conversation with Lindsay. "She acted so put out with me at first."

"She doesn't know you. And, I bet you didn't fill her in completely on the situation."

"Maybe."

"And, maybe this play thing means a lot more to her than you."

"It should. She runs the whole theater."

Leah leveled a glance at him as they walked to Brandon's room. "There you go. You and I both know what responsibility can do to a person. Don't judge her too harshly . . . at least not yet."

Pulling his sister into a hug in front of Brandon's room, he gently kissed her brow. Leah was living proof that the heavy weight of responsibility wasn't always easy to take. "Good advice. I owe it to Lindsay and the rest of the cast to at least show up. But if she gets too crazy, I'm going to quit."

Leah hugged him right back. "That's my brother, always trying to make a stand."

"Shut up." Leaning back, he examined her features. Leah looked less fragile, more like his easygoing sister. "You going to be okay?"

"Yeah. I'm going to be fine."

"I'll stop by again tomorrow."

Pushing him down the hall, she said, "I know you will, Craig. Thank you. Thanks for everything."

Chapter Eleven

Craig walked into the auditorium thirty minutes later, braced for confrontations and explanations. The conversation dissipated as he approached, making his own footsteps slow.

Lindsay turned to him as he neared the group sitting around a set of card tables on the stage. "We saved you a seat."

His steps faltered. Where was the accusing glare? The comments to everyone that he wasn't taking his role seriously? But so far, no one did a thing but smile hellos and go back to their scripts.

Craig slid in his chair between an elderly gentleman and Mrs. Mac, Dr. Stratton Sawyer's receptionist, and town curmudgeon.

Craig had learned to steer clear of her when he'd

gone to Dr. Sawyer's office for a couple of cuts and bled on one of the chairs.

"Glad you could make it, Bennett," she muttered under her breath.

He didn't dare try to figure out if she was being sarcastic or not. It didn't matter with Mrs. Mac; you never won. "Thanks."

"We're on page thirty-eight. It's moving like the dead," she whispered.

He fought a smile. "Gotcha."

As Craig settled into his spot, he got a good look around at the other occupants. About twenty-five people were sitting together, surrounding two large folding tables. Bowls of pretzels, chips, and jelly-beans were scattered around. Coffee cups and cans of soda were there, too, as well as piles of high-lighters, pencils, and Post-it notes.

Lindsay's placement surprised him. With her forthright personality, Craig was sure she'd be front and center, visibly in charge. Instead, she sat in the back, one leg propped on the back of another chair, and copiously took notes. She smiled at a couple of the actors when they looked at her for reassurance, and when one suggested a change, she nodded, and wrote something on a Post-it note.

"Bennett," Mrs. Mac hissed. "Talk."

With a start, Craig realized that the whole group was waiting on him to say his line. "Sorry. Ah, 'Mrs.

Muir, please be seated. Mr. Sproule will be with you shortly.' "

Against his will, he found himself looking toward Lindsay for approval, just like the others. She smiled and gave him a discreet thumbs-up sign.

The woman to his right wasn't nearly as generous. "Think about an English accent," Mrs. Mac said under her breath.

An hour later, Lindsay stood up. " 'The End,' " she said, doing the honors with a smile. "Well, gang, that's it for tonight. Great job." Motioning to Denise, she asked, "Any suggestions, boss?"

Denise laughed. "Not a one. I think everyone in Payton is going to love this play."

Still worried about their earlier phone conversation, Lindsay rushed over to Craig before he departed. "Would you accept an apology from me?" she asked, noticing how subdued he looked. "I'm so sorry about how I reacted to your nephew being in the hospital."

"No apology is necessary. We hardly know each other."

His words, and the cool way he spoke them, stung. Lindsay had felt they did know each other fairly well. Rather than debate their relationship, she said, "Is he going to be okay?"

"I think so." Running a hand through his golden hair, he met her gaze. "Brandon has pneumonia. Again. For some reason, he's susceptible to it—he's been in the hospital more than once with it over the last few months. It's been hard . . . my sister worries."

"I bet she does." Impulsively, she reached for his hand. When he didn't pull his hand away, Lindsay knew she wanted him to stay by her side a little longer. "Your family's lucky to have you."

"Thanks."

They were still holding hands. Lindsay wasn't anxious to let him leave anytime soon. The day had been crazy for both of them. "Do you drink coffee?"

"I do."

"Would you like to go over to the Mill and grab a cup? These first readings are usually so chaotic, there's no way I can just go to bed right away."

"Coffee sounds good."

He squeezed her hand, making her feel like they were back on even ground again. "Great! I'll just go turn off a couple of lights."

Craig watched Lindsay walk away like a kid with his first crush. Something had passed between them just a moment before. A connection. Though he'd been disappointed in her earlier lack of interest in his personal life, he had to admit he'd been charmed by her sweet apology.

As he wandered around the foyer, he noticed a breeze filtering through one of the front windows. Strange that he hadn't noticed the open window.

"Lindsay? Do you want me to close this window?" he called out, sure she did, but thinking he'd better not step on her toes.

"The window's open?"

"Yeah." He glanced toward the stairs she'd run up. Her voice had sounded funny. Almost high-pitched. "You okay?"

"Oh, sure."

Oohh-kay. Bored and antsy, he walked to the window and inspected the casing. Everything looked good. "I don't know why anyone would have opened it," he mused aloud. "There's next to no breeze, no screen." Rubbing his hand along the frame, he shook his head. "You know, come to think of it, I don't recall anyone even walking in here."

Lindsay came back into view, lines of worry creasing her forehead. "Nobody did, at least I don't think so. It might the ghost."

His hands stilled. "Who?"

"Sally."

Craig racked his brain. He'd lived in Payton most of his life, and couldn't remember ever hearing about the theater being haunted.

"Let's not talk about it right now." Smiling wanly, she said, "You ready?"

"Sure." Craig followed her out the front door and stood to one side as she locked up. Finally, they stepped out on the sidewalk together.

The air was balmy, its cool temperatures perfect for a stroll. "I do love our town's historic area. Don't you?" Lindsay remarked.

"Sure. Of course, I didn't when I was in high school. Couldn't think of anywhere less appealing."

"I grew up in a town a lot like this near Cleveland," Lindsay commented. "I used to beg Ethan to take me with him to events in the city. I guess that's normal, always wanting what you don't have."

"Yeah." They stopped at a crosswalk. When the light turned, it seemed only natural to take her hand once again. She treated him to a little smile as they stepped back on the sidewalk.

That smile was all he needed to step closer and wrap his arm around her shoulders. She felt good next to him, warm and affectionate. Right.

After briefly laying her cheek on his arm, she murmured, "I guess I should tell you more about Sally."

At the moment, he didn't care what they talked about, as long as she remained right by his side. "Only if you want to."

She peeked an eye up. "Promise you won't run away and skip out on the play?"

"Now I'm really intrigued." When she continued to wait, he teased, "I promise."

"Okay. So, like I said, Sally's a ghost."

He chuckled. "Do I look that gullible?"

"Not at all. I didn't think I was gullible either, but certain things have happened to make me think the place might actually be haunted."

Craig felt like he was free-falling into a *Twilight Zone* movie. Squeezing her shoulder, he asked, "Care to tell me why someone who seems so put together believes in ghosts?"

"There's nothing to believe or not believe. It's simply a fact. She came with the theater."

"Are there cameras around here? Are we on some reality show?"

"Ha-ha. I'm serious! Denise discovered her when she inherited the old theater last year from her Aunt Flo. I guess Sally McGraw was once an actress on the stage. She was wrongfully accused of stealing money, then accidentally met her death right in the theater."

"Has anyone figured out why she's haunting the place?"

"Not that I know of. Denise cleared her name. She said ever since then, Sally's been more of a friendly spirit. I'm fairly used to her now. Well, kind of."

"What does she do?"

"Opens windows. Plays old music on the boom box." She waved her hand. "That kind of thing. Most of our cast members are kind of fond of her."

Craig held open the door of the coffee shop for her as she walked through. "I'm kind of surprised you can talk about this all so matter-of-factly."

She looked at him in surprise. "Oh, I didn't used to feel that way. When my brother warned me about Sally, I thought he was joking." As they took a table by the front picture window, she added, "I still can't believe it."

"I guess not."

After a minute or two, they ordered cappuccinos. "Tell me about you," Lindsay said. "How did you get into construction?"

"It's all I've known. All I've ever really wanted to do," he admitted. "My grandfather had his own construction business. My father worked for him. Now I'm working for Payton Construction and doing a little bit of specialty work on the side." He shrugged. "It's a good fit for me. I like being outside. I like working with the other guys. I like the freedom it gives me."

"I can't imagine you working at a desk."

He couldn't either. "And wearing a tie? No way."

"What about your family?"

"We're a close bunch. My dad died of heart disease two years ago. All of us kids have tried to make things easier on my mom. It's been hard, though."

Lindsay sipped her drink as she watched a wealth of emotions play across Craig's features. The matter-of-fact way he described his efforts to help his mom made her heart go out to him. "You're a caring person," she said, though her description sounded small to her own ears.

He shrugged, as if embarrassed. "I do care, enough to try and do everything I can. Sometimes it's too much. I've been known to take on too much and then nothing gets done well."

She found his modesty intriguing. "Would your family say the same thing?"

"I don't know." He smiled. "Probably not. They're like anyone else . . . they don't want to look for faults in good intentions."

Lindsay thought of her own parents. They'd done a lot for her. They'd been there to help celebrate all of her accomplishments. She'd known that her parents didn't have the financial means to fund all of her dreams, so she'd worked hard in high school to earn scholarships to help pay for college. She'd volunteered for summer theaters in order to develop a reputation.

Each little step had paid off. The best part was her parents' excitement to share these things with her. Excitement that had nothing to do with her particular accomplishments—they'd had no interest in the directors who took her on, or the nature of the awards she'd received. All they'd care about was that she was happy.

"Well, I'm awfully glad you had a caring nature the day we met," she said. "I don't know what I would have done if you hadn't been there to help me out."

"Someone else would have helped you. You were really banged up." He shook his head. "Walking through a construction site in a daze. You're lucky that board didn't hit you in the head."

She winced. "Maybe it would have knocked some sense into me?"

Very gently, he brushed his fingers through her hair. "No one needs help in that way."

His fingers felt incredibly good against her head. His touch was special, as was her reaction to it. "Would you be upset if I told you that I'm kind of glad that the board hit me? If it hadn't, we would've never met."

His fingers continued to stroke. "Would you be mad if I said I'm glad we met, but I wish it would have happened another way?"

She pretended to consider. "Actually, I think I like your way better."

He laughed, fine lines framing his eyes. "Good." Leaning forward, he clasped her hand. "So, are you glad you decided to give us a try?"

Lindsay felt completely flustered. "Yes. Of course."

He leaned closer, their foreheads almost touching. "Luckily for me, we're on the same page now."

"Luckily."

His gaze flicked to her mouth. She bit her lip.

He grinned. "I like you."

The simple, unvarnished statement meant far more to her than a book of flowery statements. She'd learned that Craig did nothing, said nothing without forethought and complete honesty. "I like you too," she replied, just as honestly. Just before he finally did what she'd been hoping he would do since the moment she met him.

His head bent down. She lifted her chin. Their lips brushed against each other. Kissed. Once, twice. Finally, in earnest.

And it was just as sweet as she had hoped it would be.

Chapter Twelve

Lindsay leaned against the counter in Ethan's hardware store two weeks later. "Are you *sure* you don't want a part in the play? I'm sure you'd have fun."

"Positive."

"Come on, E," she wheedled. "Craig's in it."

"Craig is a better man than me."

With a sigh, she rested her chin in her hands and glared, though she really couldn't blame him. As much as she loved her brother, he most definitely was not the actor type.

The Ghost and Mrs. Muir was in full swing. Rehearsals had started two nights a week, and various other jobs had been assigned.

She'd been so busy working on the play and getting to know Craig that she hadn't been able to squeeze in more time to spend with Ethan. Asking him to take on a bit part was part of her desperate attempt to see him more often.

"I thought if you had a part, we could spend some time together."

Ethan continued to straighten a display on the side of his counter. "Lindsay, we don't need an activity to do that. Just come over when you can."

"I won't be able to stop by much until the play's over."

"I'll still be here." He smiled gently. "You worry too much."

"Maybe."

Unable to help herself, Lindsay reorganized the display he'd just finished. "If I can't rope you into the play, who do you think I can get for extras?"

"The Reece family."

"Really? You think any of them would do it?"

"I know they would. The whole crew of them had to get dressed up in costumes a couple of years ago for a Civil War reenactment." After writing a number on the back of a receipt, he pushed the paper toward her. "Leave my counters alone and go call up Joanne Sawyer. She can get pretty much anyone in that family to do whatever she wants." With a grin, he added, "Call her soon, that baby is due any day."

"I will." She clipped the paper to her notepad. "If you change your mind . . ."

"I won't. Linds, I've got college classes, my store, and a couple of small jobs around town. Not too mention Denise."

"Oh, don't let Denise know you mentioned her last."

He rolled his eyes. "You know what I meant."

She did. Ethan and Denise were very happy, and they seemed to have a great relationship. "Do you ever think about Mom and Dad?"

"How?"

"About how they've been married for thirty years?"

"Sometimes. In this day and age, it's commendable."

"I bet you and Denise will have a marriage like that."

"I hope so. I can't imagine life without her anymore."

His honesty made her melancholic. She hoped Denise realized just how special Ethan was. "I hope I have a relationship like that one day."

"You've got to be serious about a guy first." He paused. "Are you?"

She knew she was. Things with Craig were going well. The more time they spent together, the more they were finding they had common interests, though their relationship hadn't become too serious. "Maybe."

"Craig?"

"Yes." To her embarrassment, Lindsay felt her

cheeks heat up. "I've just got to make sure that we both want the same things out of a relationship."

"Want a little bit of advice?"

"Maybe."

"You'll know everything's right when nothing else matters. When I was falling for Denise, I no longer cared about my store as much. Or about my classes, about the gal I was casually dating . . . all I cared about was being with her, and making her happy."

"Do you think Mom and Dad were like that?"

"I'd be surprised if they weren't. Lindsay, don't get me wrong, but you have a tendency to have extreme tunnel vision. You concentrate on one thing, and one thing only. Sometimes you have to be willing to shake things up in order to make room for more. You know what I mean?"

She did. "I hear you."

"But are you ready to make changes? Lindsay, are you really ready to turn your life upside down?"

Already, she felt like she was having a hard enough time just juggling what she had. The idea of flipping everything around and to the side scared her. "Frankly, no."

"Then, maybe you shouldn't want a serious relationship."

Frustrated, Lindsay knew he was right, but she also had no idea how she was going to be able to give the time a solid relationship needed without compromising her promises. "I do want a serious relationship," she clarified. "But I don't want it to interfere with my work. I want to do a good job with this theater, for you and Denise."

Ethan stilled. "For me? What are you talking about?"

"You know, because of college and everything."

He looked completely puzzled. "I don't know what you're talking about."

"I owe you. You worked while I got to go to school."

"I'm going to school now."

"That's not the same. I've felt—I do feel that I've been given opportunities you never had. You've always been there for me, Ethan."

He squeezed her hand. "You're my little sister. Of course I'm going to be there for you."

"I don't want to let you down."

Ethan stared hard at her before finally shaking his head. "You would never let me down. Even if the theater failed, you wouldn't let me down. I'm proud of you."

"But—"

"I wasn't ready for college," he admitted quietly. "I asked Mom and Dad to let me wait. Your goals were a good reason for us all to do that."

"I never knew that."

"You didn't need to." With a sigh, he added,

"Things happen the way they do for a reason, Linds. If I had gone to college right away, I never would have worked in this store, never would have taken it over . . . never would have met Denise."

"I never thought about it that way."

"Start. I'm happy with how things are. You be happy too."

Tears pricked her eyes as she processed his words. "I love you," she said.

"You better." Kissing her on the head, he teased, "I'm the only brother you've got."

"When you asked me over for dinner, I thought we'd eat," Craig grumbled as Lindsay led him to the back of the theater.

"We will be eating. I just need your help moving some of these speakers around first. I tried to lift them earlier, but didn't get very far."

Reaching down, he lifted one handily and placed it against the wall. "Don't try again. You're going to hurt yourself. Each one has got to be sixty pounds."

"Would you be offended if I said I like watching you lift them?"

After he placed the second one by her designated wall, he waggled his eyebrows. "Would you be offended if I told you that I like watching you, no matter what?"

Her heart skipped a beat as he took her hand and

pulled her closer, something that seemed to be happening with astonishing regularity. "I wouldn't be offended in the slightest," she said, linking her arms around his neck.

His blue eyes warmed and darted to her lips.

Lindsay's pulsed raced. Ever since the time they'd discussed their relationship, they'd been flirting enough to give a junior high teen a run for his money. Though they'd kissed again, each touch had been tame.

She'd wanted more and she could tell that Craig did too.

With a lazy motion, he brushed her cheek with the pad of his thumb. "Have I ever told you that I like how you don't wear any makeup?"

Feminine wiles kicked in. "I do so. Mascara and lipstick."

"I've never noticed any. I like how you look natural, not all made-up." Fingering her ponytail, he murmured, "I like your hair too."

"I've been thinking maybe I should cut it. It just hangs there."

"It doesn't. Don't change a thing. I think you're perfect the way you are." Smiling devilishly, he added, "Especially those legs of yours. I've dreamed about your legs."

The idea made her smile. "Really? You dream about me at night?"

"Sometimes. Of course, not as much as I've dreamed of doing this," he murmured as he leaned toward her.

Their lips touched, his mouth gentle and firm and sweet. Everything she'd learned his kisses could be. She reached up and wrapped her arms around his neck, pressed a little closer into the comfort of his arms.

She was thrilled when he kissed her again, tilting his head, deepening their connection.

This was completely different than anything that had passed between them before. This kiss held promises, and spoke of futures; it propelled their relationship to a whole new level.

With reluctance, he pulled back. "Maybe this is why we don't kiss very much."

Still living in her dream world, she murmured, "Why?"

" 'Cause I don't want to stop."

She knew the feeling. But, she also knew that stopping would definitely be a good idea. Neither of them had started a discussion about their future.

"Maybe one more," he said, wrapping his arms around her waist and tugging her closer.

Lindsay met his lips, and was just thinking that maybe talking was way overrated when "In the Mood" clicked on.

Craig pulled away in confusion.

"It's not me, it's my ghost," she said, trying not to laugh.

He shook his head. "Don't tell a soul, but I'm beginning to believe in her too. She's better than a chaperone!"

"I think that's what she's trying to be. So, dinner?"

"You really are going to feed me? You didn't ask me over just to move furniture?"

"No more furniture moving. I promise." Feeling smug, she said, "For your information, I made lasagna. I have salad, garlic bread, and ice cream for dessert."

"I'm slowly beginning to realize that you have an incredibly hard time doing anything halfway." As they walked up the stairs, he teased, "What do I have to do to deserve this dinner? Memorize lines?"

Feeling happy and a little daring, she said over her shoulder, "Kiss me again."

A slow smile lit his expression. "I think I can handle that."

Chapter Thirteen

"Every night for the last month, I've seen you run out of here like your car's on fire. Where've you been going?" Jack asked as they were gathering their tools at the end of the day.

The house was almost done. All they had left to do was trim work, cabinet installation, and painting. If things went as planned, they'd move on to the next project in a week.

Craig couldn't believe how time had flown by. It was now October, and his days were busy with work, time with Lindsay, and play practice.

The weather had gotten cooler. Brightly colored red and yellow leaves covered every available surface, flying up in the air when his truck drove along Payton's windy roads.

Just the week before, they'd all gone to visit Joanne and Stratton Sawyer, and their new baby boy, Eric Samuel Sawyer.

Time had definitely moved on, but some things were still the same. No way was he going to tell Jack about his part in the play. "Nowhere special. Out."

"With the leggy blonde?"

She was so much more than that. Striving to keep his voice even, he said, "With Lindsay, yes."

"She sure is pretty."

"She is."

"So . . . things getting serious?"

"A little bit." Actually, to him, things were getting very serious. She was the only woman he wanted to spend time with, the only woman he wanted to think about being with in a month, in a year.

Just that morning while he was shaving, he'd even thought about a lifetime with her.

The idea had been so pleasant, so good, so different than how he'd ever felt about Pam, that he'd left his apartment grinning from ear to ear.

Lindsay, on the other hand, was sending mixed signals. They kissed every night. They'd even forgotten themselves a time or two and had allowed things to heat up. Craig was sure that she felt secure in his arms, and found him attractive.

But emotionally, Craig didn't feel that they'd made too many strides forward. When he compared their relationship with Leah and Jerry's constant emotional give and take, Craig felt like he and Lindsay were eons from a real, long-lasting commitment.

Jack threw a couple of scrap pieces of wood on the pile to the right of the house. "You going ring shopping soon?"

"No. Neither of us is into taking things fast."

"Fast? You two have been dating almost two months. You guys are glacial! I know, how about you bring her over on Sunday night? We'll grill some chicken. She could meet Maggie."

"That would be fun, but Lindsay's pretty busy. She runs that theater, you know."

"I've seen your truck over there. What do you do while she's working on her plays?"

Craig struggled to not lie outright. "A lot of standing around and waiting, if you want to know the truth. Lift things."

"Sounds boring."

"It's not so bad."

"Well, talk to her about coming over. The four of us would have a great time together."

Craig was sure that they'd all get along, but he was in no hurry for Lindsay to tell Jack about his new career on the stage. "Thanks, but I don't think so."

"Why? You worried I'm going to say something you don't want her to know? I won't say a word about Pam."

He was worried about the opposite. Though he could privately admit that he was enjoying the whole atmosphere of play rehearsals, no way was he going to let any of his friends know that. "I do want us all to go out together, but not yet."

Jack shrugged. "All right, whatever. At least Pam liked being around your friends," he chided as they walked out to their trucks.

Pam had been easily molded. "Pam liked whatever I liked."

"Does Lindsay?"

"Sure. We watched the Bengals game the other day. We went bike riding too."

As Craig locked his toolbox in the back of his truck, he wondered if Jack had a point. Maybe it was time to bring things to the next level. It would be good for both of them to do things with friends.

Would she care if he asked her to keep his involvement in her play a secret?

"Okay, everyone. Take a seat. Exactly two weeks from today, a hundred people will be sitting in here watching *The Ghost and Mrs. Muir.*"

Moans resounded in the theater. "It's going to be tight, Linds," Denise said from the spot in the first row. Pointing to her notepad, she added, "I've got a list of at least a dozen things that need to be done before we can pull up the curtain."

"I know. Everyone needs to have all their lines memorized by next week or face my wrath. Final costume fittings will take place this coming Sunday night."

She looked at Mrs. Reece. "How are ticket sales and promotions going, Daphne?"

"Very well. Already, opening night is sold out."

A smattering of applause, followed by a barrage of anxious conversation followed. Lindsay felt the same way. Nerves, as expected, were starting to take over, giving everyone a much needed adrenaline boost, yet also making everything seem more authentic. Everything they'd been doing and planning had an absolute purpose. And a very tight time frame.

"I feel that Act I is going well," Kim said from her chair on the stage. "I'm not too happy with the pacing of the ending, though. I'd like everyone who's involved with the last five scenes in Act II to stay here."

Lindsay nodded in complete agreement. She'd been thinking the same thing, but had worried that she was being excessively critical. "Sounds good." Looking at the cast, she said, "Sorry, everyone, but everyone who's in those scenes needs to get in position. We're going to have to go through it all one more time."

"It's going on ten o'clock, Lindsay," Jonah said.

"I know. And, I'm sorry, but there's no other time. We need to figure out what's wrong."

More grumbling and shuffling commenced again.

Unable to help herself, Lindsay looked at Craig. His character wasn't in the last of the scenes, and selfishly, Lindsay wished he was. He was so steady and sweet, just his presence seemed to make everything better for her.

As he approached, his lips turned up. "I'm going to get on out of here."

Disappointment surged through her. Valiantly, she pushed it back. "Oh. Okay."

Linking his fingers through hers, he explained. "Brandon asked me to go to a thing at his school tomorrow morning. I'm going to go to work extra early so I don't have to cut my hours."

"You better do that, then."

"You understand?"

They walked toward the back door as Kim began running the scenes. "Completely. I know you've got your own life, Craig."

Something serious flickered in his eyes. "Maybe we need to talk about that. I'd like you to meet my family. My friends."

"As your girlfriend?"

"Yes."

Pleasure rushed through her. Obviously, Craig felt the same as she did about strengthening their relationship. "I'd like that."

"So, Saturday night? It's a date?"

"Sure."

He squeezed her hand and kissed her much too briefly. "I'll call you later."

As Lindsay watched him leave, she fought the urge to chase after him, to forget the play and all of her responsibilities for a few minutes.

With a start, Lindsay realized that Craig, and her relationship with him, was starting to come first, just like Ethan had said it would one day.

The revelation was both scary and delightful.

"Lindsay, help!" Kim called out.

With effort, Lindsay turned her back to the door and Craig's departing form. "I'll be right there. Just give me a sec," she replied.

With a deep sigh, Lindsay did her best to get back on track. Now was not the time to be thinking about love. She just hoped the right time would be one day soon.

Chapter Fourteen

Dinner with Craig's family was a lot like going to the Reeces' except that she was under constant scrutiny. His four siblings, and Sandra, his mom, all asked her questions. Each answer seemed to be an indication about whether she deserved to be Craig's new girlfriend.

Lindsay had a feeling she was coming up wanting.

"So, you're the manager of the Payton Stage Company, Lindsay?" Leah asked.

"Actually, it's called the Sally McGraw Theater, but yes."

"I got really caught up in the history of that place when the *Payton Registrar* was highlighting it," Sandra said.

"It is a special old building," Lindsay agreed. "My brother did an excellent job refurbishing it."

"It must have been quite an undertaking."

"Oh, it was," Lindsay agreed. "Ethan had to do a lot of the work by hand. It turned out well, and on time."

"We didn't get to see *Scrooge*," Leah said.

"It was a great success," Lindsay smiled, thinking of how hurried they'd all been with the rehearsals . . . and then so proud when the whole audience had stood up and applauded after the first curtain call. "This next play's sure to be good too."

Leah glanced at Craig, and the way he seemed to be looking anywhere but at Lindsay. "Have you told the rest of the family what you've been doing?"

"No."

Lauren, looking every bit the preppy college co-ed she was, leaned forward. "What's Craig been doing?"

"I've got a part in the play."

The whole family burst into laughter.

"Yeah, right, Craig," Curt said. "What else have you been doing? Going to the moon?"

Lindsay felt completely confused. "He has been in the play."

More laughter followed.

"You all hush." Mrs. Bennett smiled too. "I think acting would be great fun." Looking at her kids, she added, "I've always told you all that sports and work aren't the be-all and end-all. Craig, one day you really should be in a play."

"It's not a joke," Leah said.

"I'm playing the part of assistant to Mr. Sproule. I've got seven lines," Craig added.

As the room exploded in laughter yet again, Lindsay felt her cheeks heat. She'd never been especially good in social situations—it was far easier for her to direct casts of characters—so maybe that was why she felt as if they were laughing at her occupation.

"What happened, Craig?" Lanie asked. "Did you get blackmailed into it?"

"No," Lindsay retorted. "He tried out all on his own."

"I've never known Craig to do anything without a reason. What's this one?" his brother asked.

He swallowed hard. "None of your business."

Attempting to come to his rescue, Lindsay spoke up. "Craig, I thought it was so you could be more involved in the community."

He shrugged. "It was, kind of."

"But why else?" Lauren asked.

Craig shrugged. "I tried out so I could get to know Lindsay better."

"Now isn't that sweet," Mrs. Bennett declared.

"I thought you wanted to get more involved in

Payton? To do more than just work and be with your family." The minute the words were out, she felt like she'd just let another dark secret out. "I'm sorry," she said, jumping up. "I guess I completely misread everything."

"No. No, you didn't." Craig turned to his mom. "Remember that time we ate spaghetti, and we talked about Dad's tools?"

"I do."

"Well, the next day was auditions. I wanted to get to know Lindsay better."

"And you hadn't had a life," Leah interjected. "Sit down, Lindsay. We're not trying to be mean. We were just surprised, that's all."

"It's just the last thing we'd ever expect him to do," Curt added. "Craig's kind of shy."

"Not onstage."

"I have seven lines," Craig clarified. "Plus, I stand behind a table. It's been fun."

"So why did you keep it a secret?"

"I didn't want to be subjected to all this."

"Well, Lindsay Flynn, I salute you," Lauren said, raising her glass. "If you can get Craig to come out of his shell, there's definitely more to you than a lot of long hair."

Lindsay frowned as she yanked on her ponytail. "I've been meaning to cut—"

Craig stilled her words with a kiss, right there in

front of his whole family. "Please don't. I love your hair."

Mrs. Bennett sniffed. "I'm so glad you came by, Lindsay. I have a feeling we're going to be very close, very soon."

Still stunned by the conversation and Craig's kiss, Lindsay could only nod.

Later that night, he walked her to her door. "Are you mad at me?"

"No."

"Sure?"

"I'm sure. With your family, I can see how you might not want to open yourself up to their observations."

He chuckled. "They don't hold a thing back."

"I know we're different, and but I hope you're not embarrassed about my interests."

"I'm not. I've just been eager to keep what's been between us private."

She edged up to the door. "Now everything's out in the open."

He brushed his lips against her neck. "It is."

She raised her head to meet his lips. "One day we'll have to talk about the future."

"I hope so," he murmured, just before their lips met.

When they finally came up for air, she held onto his shoulders for support. "See you tomorrow. Please tell your mom thanks again."

"I will."

"I think our relationship is getting stronger every day," she murmured, so happy to be wrapped in his arms. So happy that so many things with them were strong and solid.

A ghost of a smile lit Craig's face. "I know it is," he replied, just before their lips met once again.

Chapter Fifteen

"Ten minutes!" Lindsay called out to the sixty people milling around in the green room and auditorium of the theater. "In ten minutes, we're doing a run-through of the play, no stopping."

Turning to her stage manager, she said, "Kim, you ready?"

Kim pointed to the small cart next to her. On it was a script, a stopwatch, and about a thousand pages of notes. Also a box of tissues and a bottle of water. "Ready. I'll make note of the times and report at the end of Act I."

Lindsay checked her own notes. She also had the schedule written down, with the timing of each scene in bold highlighted numbers. "Good. If we're more than five minutes off, see if you can pinpoint what the holdup was."

"I'll do my best."

Glancing at the large clock on the back wall, Lindsay called out, "Eight minutes."

"Hey, boss, does that mean you have time to say hello?"

She turned to Craig and couldn't help but smile. "Hello."

"Hi. Are you mad at me? You didn't return my calls yesterday."

Recalling their kisses, she looked at him in surprise. "I'm not mad. Things have been crazy around here. When I could call, I knew you were at the building site. Then later, I had to go through everything with the board of directors."

He rubbed her arm. "Remember how I told you that a couple of years ago I was in a car accident?"

How could she forget? "I do."

"I made myself promise to be everything I could to people who matter. You matter, Lindsay. You matter to me very much."

Oh, he was so dreamy. "You matter to me too. I know I should have called you back, if only to leave a message," she admitted. "When this play is over, I'm going to do my best to put my priorities in perspective."

"You sure you want to wait that long? How about we go out or do something after this crazy rehearsal?"

Before, Lindsay would have said she planned to stay up until the wee hours of the morning dissecting the play. Now, she didn't feel that it mattered all that much—at least not as much as Craig mattered. "That sounds nice," she said softly.

"Good." A hint of a smile lit Craig's eyes as he leaned in and brushed his lips across hers.

Something had happened between them at his mother's house. More likely, something had happened to her. Hearing him admit to how he'd been willing to see her even though their relationship would be a surprise to his family made Lindsay want to risk more to be with him. As she recalled Ethan's fateful words, about love coming first in his life, she began to finally have a real inkling of what he meant. "Do you have any ideas of what we should do?"

"Yes." Craig didn't even attempt to hide his pleasure. "It's Friday night. Let's go to the Payton High School football game."

Doing something that had nothing to do with the theater did sound fun. "Won't it have already started?"

"Sure, but it will still be going strong at nine o'clock. We'll get some hot chocolate, wear orange and black, and cheer for the team."

"I'd love to."

Kissing her on the cheek, he leaned closer. "Five minutes."

She blinked.

"Make the announcement, Linds . . . your cast awaits."

For the first time ever, Lindsay rushed the rehearsal. She let missed lines slide and wrong cues go with just a simple warning.

She shrugged when Kim announced that one scene was six minutes too slow. She bit off a giggle when Craig said his lines with the enthusiasm of a statue.

For the first time, she was thinking about the play as a job. A fun job, a job she cared a lot about. But, a job all the same. As the last scene ended and the curtain shakily closed, she stood up.

"It's Friday night, everyone. I really appreciate you coming out and giving it your all, but I think we all need a break."

A smattering of applause greeted her words, as well as a few exclamations of surprise.

"I've written some notes about tonight's performance, and while there are some areas for improvement, there are also a lot of things we are doing well. We'll go over them at two o'clock on Sunday. Does that sound okay to you, Kim?"

"Definitely. If I leave now, I'll still be able to see my kids before they go to sleep."

"Great. It's a wrap, everyone. Have a good night.

Be here at one-thirty on Sunday. We'll begin again promptly at two. Good night."

Excited chatter erupted again.

"That's it?" Mrs. MacClusky called out. "Don't you want to meet with us individually?"

"Not tonight. I'm going to the football game."

"Well, my goodness," Denise said, stepping forward. "My very own director is going out on a Friday night?"

"Yes!" Lindsay was so happy, she didn't even attempt to justify it like she normally would have.

Denise looked at Craig. "Is he responsible for this?"

"He is."

"Good for you, Lindsay. Go get changed, I'll lock up for the night."

"You sure?"

"It's still my theater. I'm sure."

That was all the encouragement Lindsay needed. "I'll be right back, Craig," she called to him, then hastily ran up the three flights of stairs to her apartment. Off went her tobacco-colored skirt, on went comfy jeans and a black long-sleeved T-shirt. Digging out a black chenille sweater for her shoulders, she pulled on boots, then ran back downstairs.

In the small amount of time, Denise had almost everyone gone, and was chatting with Craig. "You were fast," Denise said.

Lindsay felt her cheeks heat. "I didn't want Craig to have to wait any longer."

With a knowing look, Denise smiled. "Have a good time. See you Sunday."

Craig waved bye, then pulled her out to his truck. "You look almost excited to be leaving this place."

"Don't tell anyone, but I am."

They chatted about the play the rest of the way, then walked the few blocks to the high school stadium. After quickly buying tickets from the near-deserted ticket booth, they hiked up the small hill to the stadium.

It seemed half the town of Payton was there. Orange and black decorated anything that wasn't moving, and the majority of the attendees were wearing the same colors. Teenagers of all sizes milled in the area near the snack bar, their cell phones blinking as they text-messaged each other fast and furiously.

On the field, a band played. "It's only half-time," Craig announced. "How about some hot chocolate?"

The drink sounded good. Though the air was too warm for blankets or wool coats, there was enough of a chill in the air to welcome something warm. In short order, Craig bought their drinks and led them to the adults' section. After much stair climbing and sliding, they finally sat down next to each other, just as the crowd roared to life and the Payton Panthers charged back in the stadium.

Lindsay jumped to her feet and clapped with everyone else. She couldn't help but grin at Craig as the cheerleaders yelled a complicated cheer and two elderly people next to her and Craig echoed it from their seats. All the activity and laughter made Lindsay realize that it had been a very long time since she'd enjoyed something so much.

"I can't believe you've lived here almost a whole year and never made it to a game."

"I can't believe it either."

"Let's plan on going to the next one too," he whispered in her ear.

Lindsay thought that sounded like a fine idea. "We could even tailgate."

As the band played the fight song, the cheerleaders did a routine. Half the students were on their feet with their arms raised during kickoff. Enthusiastically, Lindsay joined in.

Craig slipped an arm around her shoulders. "I'm glad you said yes and came out with me."

"Remind me to say yes more often."

"Anytime."

His lips found hers just as the team kicked a field goal.

Chapter Sixteen

"They should have won," Jack moaned, still talking about the Payton Panthers on Monday when they ran into Ethan's store to pick up a couple of tubes of caulking and wood glue.

Craig wholeheartedly agreed. "I know. The coaches should have tried for a field goal instead of running it in. And then the quarterback made the lousy pass. But what can you do?"

Ethan leaned his elbows on the counter. "The paper said it was a fumble, fair and square. But it still stinks. Here's your order," he said, pointing to a brown paper bag on the counter. "Your supervisor called it on his cell a couple of minutes ago."

"Can I charge it to the company?"

"Yep. It's already taken care of. Just sign here," Ethan said, pushing forward a slip of paper.

Craig signed and grabbed the bag from the counter. "We'll see you, E."

"See you. Hey, good for you for getting Lindsay out into the fresh air," Ethan said. "Sometimes I think days go by before she steps out of that theater."

Remembering how Lindsay cheered and clapped, Craig smiled. "We had a good time."

"Lindsay's your sister, right?" Jack asked Ethan.

"She is."

"She must be pretty special. The big guy here hasn't let me meet her," Jack said. "Maggie and I couldn't make it to the game and Craig's been dodging my invitations to dinner. I've been trying to invite them over for a month."

Ethan grinned. "You probably don't want to meet her anytime soon. She's usually going nuts right about now, with the play and all." Raising a brow to Craig, he said, "You guys will be done soon, huh?"

Craig nodded. "The play's in a couple of days."

"Have I told you that I can't wait to give you grief? Lindsay's been doing nothing but rubbing it in how you're going to be onstage and I'm not. She's completely forgotten how I helped get that building into shape."

As he glanced at Jack, Craig shifted uncomfortably. "Well—"

But Jack had already zeroed in on Ethan's words. *"On stage?* What's he talking about?"

If Craig could have slapped a hand over his buddy's mouth, he would have. "Nothing."

Ethan raised a brow. "Nothing? Lindsay said you've got your lines down pat, Bennett. In my book, that's impressive."

"Wait a minute." Turning to Craig, Jack said, "Do you mean that have a *part* in the play? You're *acting*?"

The way Jack said *acting* sounded like Craig might as well have been doing a Chippendale's number, right in the town square, which, of course, was why he'd been doing his best to keep the whole thing a secret from his construction buddies. They teased each other enough without having added ammunition. "Yep."

"How come you didn't tell me?"

"You know why. I would have never lived it down." When Jack had the nerve to look hurt, Craig slapped his shoulder. "Come on."

Jack chuckled. "Sure, we would've given you grief, but it's kind of cool too."

Ethan nodded. "I've never had the guts to act."

Craig moaned. No way was he going to become the "acting nut" in the crew. Guys would be calling him all kinds of names for years to come.

John Anderson was still getting teased about taking dancing lessons two years ago. "It's no big deal," he said quickly. "I'm not into acting, or even the play. I only did it to get to see Lindsay more often. Don't say a word to any of the guys."

"Too late," Jack shot back. "We're going to get mileage out of this for years."

"Shut up. I had to do it. Lindsay wouldn't go out with me otherwise," Craig explained, moving away from Ethan.

Jack whistled low. "What kind of woman is she? Where's your pride?"

Ethan looked up at that. "Hey," he said.

But Jack, on a serious roll, just kept talking. "So, are you going to be in her next play?"

The way Jack asked made Craig feel like a wimp. "No way. I hate standing up in front of everyone."

"I just can't believe you'd lower yourself for this girl."

"I'm not lowering myself—"

"I mean, you've never seemed the artsy type to me," Jack added, with enough of a gleam in his eye that Craig wasn't sure if he was serious or joking.

"I'm not. I just like girls who are."

Ethan winced. Gesturing toward the backdoor, he said, "Maybe you better know that Linds—"

"Is right here," she finished.

Craig groaned. Ethan covered his face with a wide, capable palm. Jack whistled low.

Arms crossed over her chest, Lindsay looked mad enough to take on all three of them with one of the wooden mallets she was standing next to. "Craig Bennett, were you too embarrassed to tell *anyone* you are in my play?"

Since that was about right, he backpedaled in a way that would make Lance Armstrong proud. "I told some people. I told Leah."

She shook her head. "I guess I should be grateful for that."

"Why are you upset?" He stepped forward. "You aren't seriously upset, are you?"

Lindsay narrowed her eyes. "Maybe."

Ethan winced again before stepping out from behind the counter. "I think I'll go in the back room," he mumbled before dodging out of sight.

Craig tried again to diffuse the situation. "I wish you would have let me know you were here."

"Really? It sounds to me that I shouldn't have been doing a lot of things . . . like dating certain construction workers." Craig reached for her hand—anything to get back the contact he'd enjoyed with her. But before he could get within a foot of her, she stepped back.

"Lindsay, let's go talk about this," he coaxed, not even caring that Jack was still standing near.

She shook her head. "No. Way."

"We need to. I'll talk to you tonight at practice."

"Whatever."

Her apathy, so different than her usual enthusiasm, worried him. "Baby—"

"Don't call me that." She backed away.

"Lindsay, don't be mad," Craig cajoled.

"I appreciate how you're acting in the play to be with me. But, it hurts to hear it sound like you've hated every minute of it."

Jack crossed his arms over his chest. "Hey, I'm sorry I brought all this up."

Lindsay shook her head. "No, it's not your fault. I was wrong to think two such different people could ever have very much in common." Facing Craig, she said, "Go build something. Do something that your friends and family will approve of."

Like a mini-tornado, she was gone. Both men watched her open the door, slam it shut, and storm away.

Jack whistled low. "Wow, Bennett. She's pretty amazing. And what a set of legs."

Ethan came out of the back room just in time to hear the last comment. "It's probably time you went on your way," he said.

As Craig watched Jack leave with their sack of supplies, he leaned against the corner of a gardening display.

Lindsay was gone.

He felt like he'd just been tarred, feathered, and

left for road kill. All of the times he'd had with her floated through his mind. Their first kiss. The way she lit up as she ordered people around during play practice.

The time she laughed uncontrollably when they'd all messed up their lines, and she'd realized she'd Xeroxed the parts wrong.

The way she'd told him she was so grateful that he was willing to try something new just to spend time with her.

The way she'd gone to the game, cheered like crazy for the Panthers, and confided that she couldn't wait until the next game.

And now she—and his bit part in *Ghost* that he'd even been kind of excited about—was gone.

Staring at the entrance of the store, thinking that his future had just ran out on him, Craig murmured to Ethan, "Got any advice?"

"Maybe. See the door? Use it. Go make up with Lindsay. I learned from Denise that being with the woman you love means more than anything else in the world."

Craig stared at him. Never had he heard a guy speak about love like that.

But Ethan obviously thought he was moving too slow. "Bennett. Do you love her?"

The truth hit him like a sack of nails. "Yeah. I do."

"Then maybe you ought to tell her."

Craig was a lot of things, but a fool wasn't one of them. "Bye," he said, ready to go find Lindsay . . . and tell her exactly how he felt.

"Lindsay, wait up!"

Turning from her mad dash along the bike path, she spied Craig loping toward her. "I think it's best if we don't talk right now," she said over her shoulder.

"I think you're wrong. Stop, will you?"

Her feet slowed.

"Thank you," he gasped, panting. "I was about to have a heart attack."

She had no desire to joke about anything with him. "Craig—"

He grabbed her hands. "Listen to me. You overheard a conversation I'm not very proud of. But, you didn't hear the whole thing."

"What part did I miss? Look, Craig, I don't know what you want from me. It was embarrassing hearing from your family how you didn't want to share that you were in my play, but to hear how you really thought about my job, about everything that I'm doing . . . that was tough."

"I know."

She seriously doubted it. "Do you? Craig, this theater isn't my hobby. It's way more than just my vocation. It's a big part of who I am. I can't be with a guy who doesn't see that."

"I started to really like being there."

"That's not what you said a couple of minutes ago." Feeling frustrated with him, and with herself for forgetting that he'd only been doing the play to be with her, Lindsay softened her voice. "Look, I know plays aren't your thing. They don't have to be."

"Plays aren't my thing. You know I only tried out because I wanted to be with you. I was willing to get on stage because I wanted to see you. But, I did mean it when I said I've been having a good time."

Lindsay didn't know what to think. She was humbled that he was willing to do so much to be with her . . . yet she didn't know what the right thing to do was.

"I'm still the same guy you first met," Craig continued. "I like pizza and beer and poker with the guys and softball games. I doubt I'll ever be into wine or neckties or musicals."

"So—"

"But don't you see? I've been willing to try new things to be with you. I've been willing to do a lot to be with you, to give us a chance. Shouldn't you give us a chance too? I thought you liked me."

She might have been mad at him, but she couldn't lie about her feelings. "I do like you. You know I do."

"What about all the things we've done together, like going to the game. Did you have fun?"

"You know I did."

"Have you told all your artsy friends about me? About the guy who works with his hands for a living? Who has no plans to get a degree? Who hasn't seen any of the plays you refer to?"

"Those things don't matter. You're a wonderful person. You do so much for your family. For everyone."

"Then don't write us off." Lowering his voice, he said, "I think I'm falling for you."

I'm falling for you. A lump formed in her throat. She felt the same way, that's why she was so hurt.

And she wasn't quite ready to admit her feelings, she felt too topsy-turvy inside. "I won't write us off," she whispered. "I don't want to do that."

Rubbing a knuckle, he said, "Are you going to kick me off the play?"

Like the play was what she was worried about! "Of course not."

He squeezed her hands. "Good. Things will be better between us, Lindsay. I promise."

"I hope so too," she said with all her heart.

Chapter Seventeen

Opening night was supposed to be going more smoothly than it was, Lindsay thought to herself.

A whole lot better.

Not that things could get much worse. At the moment, Murphy's Law was in full effect—everything that could go wrong was going wrong. Two of the costumes were missing. One of the makeup artists was sick.

They'd sold too many tickets and were now trying to squeeze in ten extra chairs.

And Craig Bennett was everywhere she looked.

Oh, she wasn't mad at him any longer. Lindsay knew from being around her brother that guys talked . . . and sometimes elaborated stories. It was what guys did.

She just wasn't sure how things were going to be when the play was all over. She couldn't expect him to suddenly get parts in every play she produced.

And no matter how much time she took off in between productions, she knew she was still going to have a schedule that wasn't conducive to dating.

And then there were their differences in likes and lifestyles.

She wasn't hoping for a carbon copy of herself. But maybe someone who would at least have an understanding of her love of theater?

Kim walked up, her expression grim. "Slight problem, Linds. It's raining outside. Make that pouring outside. We're having to move the props from the staging area to behind the curtain."

Lindsay knew where that was heading. "Which, in turn, makes the actors' entrances dangerous," she finished. "Thanks, I'll look into it."

"Jonah needs someone to calm him down."

Jonah, who was playing the part of the captain, was turning into being an extremely high-maintenance kind of guy. Lindsay groaned. "I don't have time to settle him. Do you?"

"Do you think I would have brought him up if I did?"

"No. Send him over. I'll deliver his nightly pep talk."

"Thank you."

"Anything else?"

A wide smile formed on her assistant's lips. "Break a leg, boss. It's going to be a winner tonight."

"I feel that too!"

After giving Lindsay a high five, Kim disappeared backstage once again.

Just as Lindsay was sorting through her notes and double-checking the status of her cast, a window popped open.

Well, of course her crazy theater would get all "haunty" again—everything else was nutty. "Not right now," she told the empty room. "Give me a break, please?"

"You wanted to see me?" Jonah interrupted, glancing around the room in a curious way.

"I did," Lindsay replied, feeling her cheeks heat in embarrassment. "How are you feeling?"

"As nervous as a newborn chick. What am I going to do if I'm a total failure?"

"You won't be."

"Promise?"

"I've been directing you for the last two months. I wouldn't let you fail, Jonah. You know me. This theater means the world to me."

But just as the words left her, she realized something else. Craig did too.

As Jonah walked away and she was alone again, Lindsay breathed deeply.

Maybe that was why she wasn't as nervous as

usual. She already had him, and that was more important than anything else in the world.

"Three cheers to our director!" Katie, their Lucy Muir, sang out right after the cast did their final bow.

On the other side of the curtain, some of the audience was still clapping, others were laughing and talking excitedly. Lindsay took those as good signs.

Her one flop had involved stilted silence and a quiet exodus.

"Hip, hip, hooray!" Jonah yelled, followed by the chorus of the rest of the cast.

After everyone clapped, Lindsay bowed. "Thanks everyone, but we all know that you did the hard part: acting! From what I saw, it was wonderful and great. The audience loved it."

"What they saw was good," Kim clarified.

Lindsay laughed. "*Saw* is the opportune word. What the audience doesn't see or notice is just fine."

"A lot things that could have gone wrong went wrong," Kim stated. "It was crazy backstage."

"Tonight was interesting," Lindsay agreed.

Jonah groaned. " 'Interesting.' Yeah, that's the word for it."

"But we all pulled through. Thanks so much for all of your hard work. You all make my job wonderful!"

As the crew and cast burst into applause, Lindsay laughed . . . and looked for Craig. He was the one person who would make their night a complete success. But as she scanned the group of familiar faces, not a one of them was the man she'd come to love.

"Someone left this for you," Kim said, handing her a notecard. Right away, Lindsay recognized Craig's scrawled handwriting.

As she scanned the hastily written message, her heart sank. Brandon was doing poorly, his sister was in tears, and his mom was out of town.

Craig would call her tomorrow, but she might need to find someone else to play his part for the next performance.

But the part that made her gasp was his last line. He hoped she would forgive him.

Gosh, had he really thought she wouldn't?

After two weeks, the final night of *The Ghost and Mrs. Muir* was under way.

Lindsay tried to evaluate how she felt as the curtain went up for the very last time, but as she stood to the side and watched the cast get into place, she realized she had no words for her feelings.

A crazy mixture of emotions flew through her: relief that another play had gone off without a hitch; pride that everyone had been so complimentary, including Denise; sadness that so much work was about to be over . . . and would soon dissolve into memories and yearbooks. And, most importantly, a curious sense of indifference.

She'd been hurt when she'd received Craig's note, but had been afraid to comment on it because he already had enough to deal with.

She'd heard from one of his sisters that he'd been working full time, helping Leah, and just barely squeezing his commitment to perform in the play. Now, Craig arrived at the very last moment, said his lines onstage, then left soon afterward.

Never once had he asked her to visit the hospital with him, or to remove him completely from the production.

She truly missed him. His absence made Lindsay feel as if nothing really mattered anymore—not what she did, not how she did it. Everything had suddenly seemed more special when she had Craig to share it with.

Kim walked by. Lindsay gave her a thumbs-up, then leaned against the wall. Craig's scene wasn't until Act II; he was hanging outside or in the green room. Someplace far from her.

Her cell vibrated, which took her by surprise. She usually very carefully turned it off and left it in her purse, though that was usually a technicality. Everyone who knew her knew that she was busy working on the play.

Unclipping it from her waistband, she glanced at the caller ID. Ethan?

Nodding to Kim, she scooted out to the green room. The rest of the cast who weren't onstage were cracking jokes. Frustrated, she backed out the back door and into the alley. Finally able to call, she dialed his number.

He answered on the second ring.

"Ethan? What's up?"

"Don't freak out, but . . . I'm at the hospital, Linds."

She nearly dropped the phone. "What? Are you okay? What happened?"

"Crazy accident at work. I'm okay, but my wrist hurts like the devil. The doc thinks I might have broken it. I'm probably going to need a cast."

"And stitches," Denise called out.

Lindsay gripped the phone a little tighter. "Stitches? What?"

"It's nothing. I had a couple of scrapes. Look, I don't want to keep you, I know the play just started. I just didn't want you to hear it from somebody else. I'll call you later on tonight."

Immediately he clicked off.

Lindsay stared at her phone. She felt like it was a foreign object.

Had her brother really just called, informed her

that he was in the emergency room getting stitches and casts, but that he knew she wouldn't do anything because she had a play?

How awful was that?

All at once, everything that Denise, and Ethan, and Daphne Reece, and most of all, Craig, had said to her came flooding back to her. Nothing mattered but memories of people. Her family. People she loved.

She felt embarrassed and humbled. Her own brother had known that her priorities were completely misplaced.

"You okay?" Craig asked, stepping out to join her. "I saw you fly out here."

"The reception was better outside," she said through a haze. "My brother called. He's in the hospital."

Craig closed the gap between them and took her hand for the first time in days. "What's happened?"

"I'm not sure. He said there was some kind of accident. He's got a broken arm or wrist or something. Stitches."

Pulling her closer, he said, "If he can call, he's going to be okay. Is Denise there?"

"Of course she is," she replied, realizing with a start that she couldn't say the same about herself. "I need to go."

"All right," he said, not questioning her decision. "I'll take you."

"You don't mind?"

"Not at all."

"I would have visited Brandon with you, if you'd asked," she said.

Humor and compassion entered his gaze. "Thank you. Next time I'll ask."

After they took two steps, she stopped. "What about the play? What are we going to do?"

"The play's in the middle of the first act. Kim's got it under control. I can ask Pete or somebody to play my part." Shrugging, he treated her to half a smile. "We both know it mainly involves standing around and looking confused."

Still gripping his hand, she nodded. "I better go talk to Kim."

"You go find your purse and a jacket. I'll talk to Kim for you."

"Thank you, Craig."

He kissed her brow. "You're welcome."

Minutes later, Lindsay was sitting next to Craig in his truck's cab as he maneuvered the large vehicle out of the crowded parking lot and onto the rain-drenched streets. "Thanks," she said again.

"You don't need to thank me. Everything's working out."

"I know. But it might not have." She fingered the phone in her hand, which had been suspiciously silent. "Why hasn't Ethan called me again? Do you think something bad happened?"

"I think he knows that you've got a play to direct. It's where he expected you to be."

Craig's matter-of-fact statement led to an onslaught of tears. "I feel like I've been acting like a self-centered kid."

"Oh, honey," he said as he found a parking place. "Everything's going to be okay. Your brother's a tough guy."

She shook her head. "It's not that. I'm sorry about us. I very stupidly discounted all of your other obligations. I placed our relationship behind that play. It was so completely wrong."

After unbuckling his seatbelt, he pulled her to him. Lindsay automatically curved into the comfort of his arms. "You haven't done anything wrong. You're trying to juggle your life." Sheepishly, he smiled. "And, I did lie to my family about the play, and got worried when I didn't think you were ever going to put us first. My family did need me, but I also used that as an excuse to back off." Brushing a hand down her back, he said, "Let's put each other first from now on."

"I love you," she blurted. As his eyes widened, she added, "I know it's probably the wrong time and the wrong place to say this, but I don't want another minute to go by before I gather up my nerves. I love you. I love being with you. I just wanted you to know that."

"I love you too," he said softly.

Something imperceptible formed between them. Something sweet and good and long-lasting. Lindsay figured it was honesty. She liked the idea, almost as much as she liked hearing those three very simple words from him. "You don't have to say it just because I did," she whispered.

"Lindsay, I think I'm beyond the stage where I say things out of obligation. I know how I feel. And, I know I love you."

"I don't think I've ever told you how much I've appreciated everything you've done for me."

Kissing her brow, he murmured, "Tell me now."

"I app—"

"Show me." He claimed her lips before she could finish her silly apology.

Actually, he claimed her lips before she could do much but hold on and think about just how much she loved being in his arms. And how much she loved being in love with him.

And he loved her too!

Though they'd kissed many times before, everything seemed new and special. When he nibbled her bottom lip and coaxed her closer, Lindsay shivered and wrapped her hands around his neck. Coaxed her fingers through his hair, loved how good it felt to taste him, to be so close to him . . . and kiss him again.

"Tell me you're going to be okay," Lindsay demanded as soon as she got to Ethan's curtained area in the emergency room.

Ethan rolled his eyes. "I'm going to be okay. I can't believe you came to the hospital. Go on back the theater."

"I can't believe you'd think I wouldn't come see you."

"I thought you'd come by later. I figured you would know that Denise is here," he explained, linking his fingers through hers. "She's taking care of everything."

Lindsay knew that was true. The only time Denise had left Ethan's side was when he needed something. Her soft-spoken ways had soothed his temper, and she was just helping him get organized and out the door.

"After I get Ethan settled, I'm going to run by the cast party," Denise said. "Lindsay, don't you think you should go on back?"

She looked worriedly at Ethan. His arm was bandaged and surrounded by ice. He had multiple bandages on his arms and one long set of stitches near his chin. "My brother—"

"Is right here," Ethan interrupted. "I'm fine, Linds. Go on."

Reluctantly, she stepped back and let Craig take her hand. Without a word, they went back to his truck.

"I hope I made the right decision," she said after they got settled once again.

"I think you're doing everything just fine." Glancing at the clock on his dashboard, he said, "If I gun it, I bet we could make it back before the end of the show."

For a split second, she tried not to care. But she truly did. It would be awesome to be with the cast for the very last bow. "Am I a bad person if I admit to being glad about that?"

"No. You're being Lindsay."

They entered the theater at the end of the last scene. From what Kim and the rest of the cast had to say, everything was going off without a hitch. Lindsay didn't know whether to be really happy about that, or more than a little put out that she wasn't as needed as she'd previously thought.

But as the curtain fell for the final time and the audience streamed out the back doors, Lindsay hugged everyone and lavished praise. It had been a good show.

Kim announced that the board of directors was throwing them a cast party at the Payton Country Club.

After promising Craig she'd meet him there, Lindsay wandered back to the auditorium, alone.

What a day.

What a day for revelations!

She and Craig were in love, the theater had actually come in second place in her life . . . and both had been just fine.

Ethan had been hurt, and it had been his wife who made everything better, and had told Lindsay to go where she was most needed—directing the play.

A crash echoed along the back hallway. For a split second, Lindsay almost hoped it was a burglar. That she could deal with. But only the faint scent of talcum powder guided her way.

Maybe she really did have a ghost.

In case she did have someone to talk to, Lindsay said aloud, "Maybe I've been trying to find myself in the theater, in my work, in my obligations . . . when all of it has been right in front of me all along. It's just taken a while to see that.

"I've got a great job, a good brother . . . and a good man."

She was just about to step back toward the crowd when she spied herself in a cracked mirror. It was leaning against the wall haphazardly, the glass cloudy, the frame bent.

But still, if she tilted her head to one side, she could see herself looking right back.

For a long moment, she stared. Looking back at her was a pretty average-looking woman. A little taller than most. Clad in comfortable faded jeans, a white T-shirt, and black boots. As usual, her long hair was pulled out of the way in a barrette down her back.

But the woman's eyes were bright and excited. Her cheeks were flushed. She looked happy. She looked excited about the future. "Looks like you've finally found love, Lindsay," she told her reflection.

And as she walked out the door to meet Craig and the rest of the cast, Lindsay figured that love looked kind of nice on her.

Actually, it looked just about perfect.